DRAGONWÜLF
BOOK III

Drakwnúlfr

Bók III

THE AGE OF METAL

A NOVEL BY
SALVATORE DEBELLA

DRAGONWÜLF

BOOK III

Drakwnúlfr

Bók III

THE AGE OF METAL

A NOVEL BY
SALVATORE DEBELLA

DRAGONWÜLF
Book III: The Age of Metal
by **Salvatore DeBella** © 2025 Salvatore DeBella
All rights reserved.

ISBN
979-8-90329-411-4
Imprint Staten House

Printed in the United States of America

This book is a work of fiction and not a biography; while real historical figures, events, or public documents may be used, the dialogue, scenes, and interpretations of their personal thoughts or lives are invented for the purpose of the story.
Any resemblance between fictionalized aspects of the real-life person and actual events is coincidental.
Names, characters, places, and incidents are products of the author's imagination or are used fictitiously. Any resemblance to actual persons, living or dead, or actual events is purely coincidental.

Contents

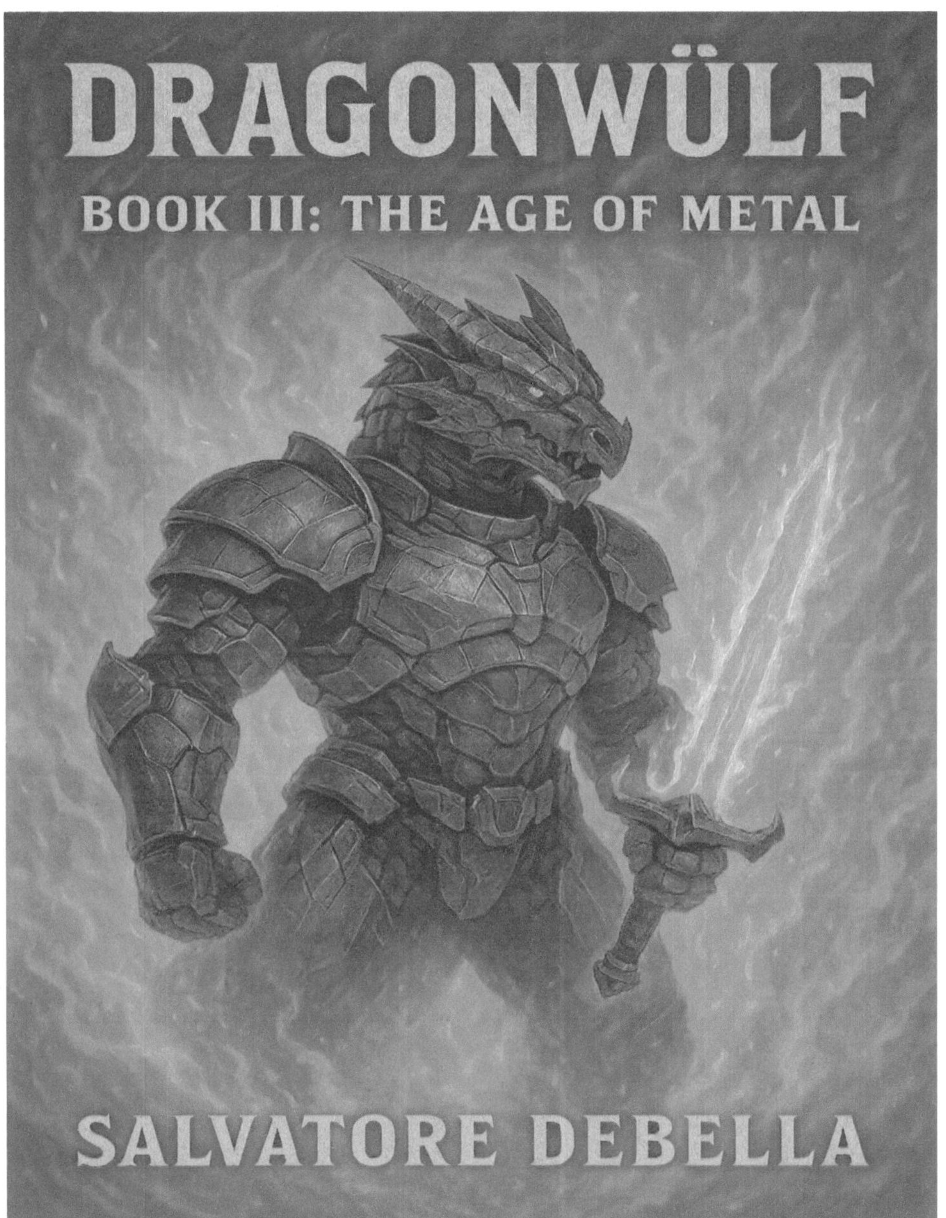

DRAGONWÜLF
BOOK III: THE AGE OF METAL
SALVATORE DEBELLA

Old Norse Translations   (poetic / saga style) Translated from the rune carvings discovered by Sir Robert Winterfall in his expeditions of the Underforest (circa 1992-1894).

Rune Carvings done in Elder Futhark Transliterations (approximated) 3rd to 8th Centuries

PREFACE

The New World

inn nýi heimr

ᛁᚻ ᛏᛁ ᚻᛗᛁᛗᚱ

Date: Future Dimension of Thor.

The culmination of the war of 2429 CE

Obedience is mercy, and defiance is art.

The mysterious schemes of dishonest men and renegade gods have thrown the world into turmoil. The records of Dr. Robert Winterfall have come into my possession. It was only a matter of time before the murderous ghoul that killed my friend would find me. The twentieth century saw the abomination of two world wars and countless conflicts. The twenty-first and subsequent centuries have fared no better, I fear.

As a continuation of the previous narrative, I have possession of the original records of Sir Robert Winterfall (1894). In addition, I have new records from the year 2429 CE. This is the year of what has been referred to as "The Final Year War."

Since *Twilight of the Gods,* I have discovered, purely by accident, a method by which I can jump from one time to another. Dr. Moreau was working on a "time machine" at the time of his death, but never perfected it. As irony would have it, he was looking in the wrong place. When I was visited by the same "being" that ended the life of Dr Moreau, I stealthily followed him to the gates of the portal.

Sir Robert Winterfall (1850-1932) formulated a concept concerning the universe and co-existing timelines. He called this the *Panorama Effect.* It can be explained by visualizing the universe and timelines as open to view from all directions. The theory states that all timelines can be examined simultaneously in real-time.

I will attempt to describe what I witnessed through the Panorama in this new record, "*The Age of Metal.*"

This is the continuation of the tale of Dragonwülf and the council of Tyr. In *Twilight of the Gods,* I told the story of the battle of The Defiler of Souls and the search to destroy him and his works. It was published as a group of artifacts collected by the late Dr. James Winterfall, the grandson of the original researcher. I will present the new artifacts in the order that I received them.

In my last jump into the Panorama, I decided to stay and witness the end of the world. That indeed turned out to be an unwise, albeit downright foolish decision. I speak with you through the corridors of time, and I hope this document reaches you, whoever you may be. It is by pure serendipity that you have this in your hands, given the fact that I am likely centuries in the grave by now.

In this, the final year of my existence, I sit upon the cusp of a new age as I pray for the coming of one who would rescue those who remain from destruction.

We await his arrival and his identity.

The Abominations of Ogor the Impaler

They learned his name before they learned how to scream.

Across the broken spiral of inhabited worlds, whispers traveled faster than fleets: *Ogor is coming.* Not a conqueror, not a general, but an instrument. A living decree of suffering sent forth by the Defiler of Souls, whose will was not domination, but erasure through pain. Ogor did not burn cities. He *humiliated* them.

He arrived on the *moon of Kareth-9* without announcement. No orbital bombardment. No negotiations. The sky simply darkened as his citadel-ship anchored itself above the capital spire, blotting out the twin suns like a judgment passed in silence.

The inhabitants gathered in confusion at first. Then fear. Then despair.

Ogor descended alone.

He was vast and way too tall, too rigid, as though his body had been built around a single purpose. His armor was ancient and blackened, ribbed with iron struts that rose from his shoulders like a cage turned outward. Behind him floated his weapons, obedient as dogs long, barbed pylons of soul-forged metal, humming softly, eagerly.

The Defiler spoke through him not in words, but in commands. Ogor knelt, not in reverence, but in reception. The work began. They never killed first. That was the rule. Ogor's victims were chosen publicly. Of course, just as all ghouls and dictators of history, they chose leaders, artists, and anyone whose suffering would echo throughout the ears of the people. All of the despots of history have done this. It is always met with surprise and even shock, but we wonder why. We have seen the same from Hitler, Stalin, Pol Pot, and Cyrus Kain from the bastardized AmeriKa. With a slow, ceremonial precision, he raised the pylons from the ground, one by one, planting them into the plazas, the temples, the halls of learning. Each spike was taller than a tower, etched with sigils that drank sound and fed on terror.

Then came the impalement.

Ogor did not rush. He positioned each victim carefully, lifting them as one might lift an offering. The spikes did not tear. The metal phased through flesh and armor alike, locking the victim in place alive, aware, unable to faint or die.

Suspended above the crowds. Breathing. Watching.

The pylons radiated pain outward, amplifying every cry into a chorus that soaked into the ground, the buildings, the air itself. The Defiler fed on that resonance. Entire worlds became instruments, tuned to agony.

Ogor walked among them as they writhed, adjusting the angle of a spike here, raising another higher there, ensuring maximum visibility. He listened not with pleasure, but with satisfaction. A craftsman admiring his work. When the screams began to fade, when hope thinned, and voices broke, Ogor activated the final rite.

The Impalers bloomed, and jagged barbs unfolded. Light twisted. The victims' shadows stretched impossibly long across the stone, writhing independently, trapped even after consciousness fled. Their souls were pinned as firmly as their bodies hopelessly nailed to reality so the Defiler could savor them at leisure. Days later, when Ogor departed, the bodies remained. Cities were left intact. Populations untouched. But everywhere one looked, there were spikes. Towers of living memory. A skyline of suffering that would never decay, never end. That was the lesson.

Obedience is mercy, and defiance is art. As Ogor returned to the void, the Defiler's presence receded, sated for now. The Impaler did not look back. He never did. Behind him, an entire world learned what it meant to be remembered by pain.

And across the universe, others heard the screams, faint, eternal, and completely understood that The Defiler did not need armies.

He had Ogor.

Artifact One

Wigmir's War

Wigmirar orrosta

ᛈᛁᚲᛗᛁᚱᚠᚱ ᛟᚱᛟᛖᛏᚠ

Date: Future Dimension of Thor 2396 CE

Saturn Moon Enceladus Colony/ the Iron Catacombs

"Lunethir lunethar zevra sora."

"The moons shine like fire upon the water." -Translation from
Encladean Tongue.

After losing the trail, The Deepwater Watchman journeyed in search of

Ogor and The Defiler. Captain Turas followed his heart and his own advice.

"When you do not know what to do, you must do what you know."

The Deepwater would have to contend with the cannibal ghoul, Ogor the Impaler, *as well* as the Defiler of Souls. They would try to follow the moon of Kareth-9. Reports of the Impaler's abominations were spread widely.

The Wake of the Impaler

The Deepwater Watchman drifted at silent burn along the torn edge of the Hadrian Expanse, its hull lights dimmed to the level of ghost fire. Beyond the viewports, the stars were wrong—bent, reddened, as if the universe itself recoiled from what lay ahead.

Dragonwülf stood at the forward observation dais, titanium gauntlets resting on the rail, unmoving. His ancient eyes—older than the ship, older than the void—tracked the debris field slowly rotating before them.

Not debris but remains.

"Confirmed," murmured Captain Old-Turas, his voice hoarse. "That's the *Aurelian Mercy* the relief vessel. Registry still broadcasting… or what's left of it."

The image sharpened. The ship had not been blasted apart. Its hull was *opened*, peeled like flesh. Long struts protruded from the central spine—steel spars driven through compartments, through decks, through bodies.

Impaled.

A low growl rolled from Dragonwülf's chest.

"Ogor," he said. It was not a question. It was a verdict.

The crew of the Deepwater had hunted warlords, slavers, void-things born of dead gods but this was different. Ogor the Impaler did not conquer. He did not raid for profit. He *performed.* Every atrocity was a message and every corpse was a signature.

"Scans show life-signs," said Lira Vance, the ship's new navigator, her fingers trembling as they danced across the console. "Faint but a few sounds. They sound agonized. Mat the Gods help them…"

"Launch rescue teams," Old-Turas ordered. "Weapons hot. No heroics."

Dragonwülf was already moving.

They found the survivors in what had once been the Mercy's sanctuary bay.

The room had been turned into a forest of agony.

Men and women aid workers, medics were fixed upright along the walls and floor by dark-metal spikes that hummed with residual warp energy. Some were dead. Some were not.

One survivor still breathed, shallow and broken, eyes glassy but aware. A spike had pierced him cleanly through the abdomen, pinning him in place like an insect in a collector's case.

Dragonwülf knelt before him.

"Ogor," the man whispered, lips cracking. "He… wanted us awake."

Rage flared bright and dangerous but Dragonwülf forced it down. He placed a massive hand over the man's heart and whispered an Old Norse prayer, one meant for warriors lost in snowstorms and battlefields.

The man smiled once. Then he was gone.

Behind them, one of the Deepwater's marines retched.

"Captain," Lira said, voice tight with terror. "We're detecting movement. Multiple heat distortions and plasma trails. He is still here."

The lights died.

Darkness swallowed the sanctuary bay.

Then…*Laughter that was d*eep and mocking. Echoing through the metal like a blade dragged slowly across bone.

"Dragonwülf," came the voice, distorted yet intimate. "Are you still chasing ghosts?"

Emergency lights flared crimson and Ogor the Impaler stepped into view.

He was enormous, even by augmented standards. His armor was a grotesque parody of knightly plate, fused with spikes, hooks, and screaming sigils that bled light. A rack of impalement rods floated behind him, orbiting like obedient beasts.

He gestured casually, and one of the spikes twisted.

A body screamed.

"STOP!" Old-Turas shouted.

Ogor's helm turned, lenses flaring.

"Oh… I will," he said pleasantly. "But not yet."

Dragonwülf charged.

The deck plates *buckled* beneath his stride. He swung his hammer in a blow that would have shattered a dreadnought but Ogor *was not there*.

The Defiler's magic rippled. Space folded. Ogor reappeared atop a broken altar, clapping slowly.

"So close," he mocked. "You follow my trail so faithfully. I should reward such devotion."

The impalement rods shot forward.

Dragonwülf deflected two, shattered a third but one struck true, pinning his cape to the wall. Power screamed through the metal, locking his suit momentarily.

Ogor leaned close.

"Tell the Council," he whispered, voice dripping delight, "that the Impaler still walks. And that the gods scream so beautifully when they realize they cannot stop me."

With a violent surge of warp-light, Ogor vanished leaving behind only the stench of ozone, blood, and failure.

The silence afterward was unbearable.

Back aboard the Deepwater Watchman, the crew worked wordlessly. Bodies were recovered. Survivors—what few there were—were sedated, wrapped in mercy and grief.

Dragonwülf stood alone in the observation bay once more, staring into the dark.

Old-Turas joined him.

"We had him," the captain said quietly.

Dragonwülf's voice was iron.

"No. We *saw* him."

He clenched his fists.

"And now the universe will know what follows."

Outside the viewport, the stars continued to bleed red as if Ogor's laughter still echoed through the heavens.

Onward Enceladus

Jarvis Nightwish claimed the Saturn Moon Enceladus Colony as his home colony and the moon of his home planet. The ice giants attacked and destroyed his world, and he must be given that chance to make it right. It was time for Nightwish to reconcile its timeline and balance his personal universe. Most importantly. This moon was the next target of Ogor the Impaler.

As the ship sailed through the cosmic ocean, the crew gathered on the deck, their eyes filled with wonder at the celestial beauty surrounding them. The Panorama engulfed and pitched the ship and crew to a period directly before the massacre of Enceladus at the hands of the ice giants. There was hope they might be able to save the innocents from the war.

"My friends," Nightwish announced, his voice carrying a sense of reverence, "This pile of rocks once was the jewel of the Saturn system, Enceladus. Prepare yourselves for a sight that will leave you breathless or underwhelmed. I am not sure which anymore."

The former colony of Enceladus was a marvel of technology and ingenuity.

"Nightwish explained, "The people had created a paradise amidst the frozen wasteland, a testament to the resilience of humankind. It was laid waste by the ice giants."

"Why did they destroy it?" asked Sir Robert.

"They wished to have the colony for a home world for the ice and frost giants," answered Nightwish. "They took that which was not theirs as if they were allowed to lay claim to it by the ancient texts of the ice people. They claim their 'god' had given them the moon as theirs to populate. They wanted to make a paradise."

Viktor Vorobyev interjected his voice gruffly with skepticism. "Paradise or not, I'll believe it when I see it. Space is full of tall tales and wild exaggerations. Earth is full of religious fantasies like that."

The ship continued its steady course toward the glistening moon. Members of the crew were lost in their own thoughts and dreams. As they drew closer, the icy surface of Enceladus loomed larger and larger, revealing hints of the thriving colony hidden beneath. "I have not been back since the destruction of my people," said Nightwish. "Before the ice giants came, the cunning ones of our people became their servants and did their bidding. They chose this path to save their cowardly skins. These weak-minded ones constructed a Temple for the worship of the Grand ice giant, and it became a way of controlling the people that remained alive. We must destroy this abomination."

Finally, the Deepwater Watchman docked at the Enceladus Colony, and the crew disembarked onto the frost-covered ground. Gasps of amazement were heard as they beheld the glittering domes and spires of the colony, bathed in the soft light of Saturn.

"I cannot believe it. It is just how I remember it," whispered Nightwish, his eyes wide with awe. "It's still more beautiful than I ever remembered," his heart swelling with emotion. "Welcome home, my friends. Welcome to Enceladus, the home of my fathers."

Dragonwülf gathered his crew in the ship's meeting room before they disembarked.

"As we land near the Enceladus Colony, crew reports have confirmed that renegade ice giants are planning an attack on the colony. Our friend *Wigmir* has met us here from the underground and has agreed to help us fight them off," said Dragonwülf.

"Wigmir," shouted a surprised Nightwish. "You are not going to believe this, but a robber I put to death many years ago on Enceladus screamed your name as he was disintegrated by the disruptor."

"What was his name? Who was this man that he deserved that?" asked Wigmir.

"He was robbing me at knifepoint. I even warned him. He was not aware that he was robbing the high executioner of the temple. I never knew his name, and I did not think to ask. He just screamed with his last breath, *see Wigmir*."

Some of the underground workers were part of the resistance against the evil ice giants. They often fed their families by pickpocketing and street robbery. No doubt he was one of them," said Wigmir.

Nightwish suddenly felt sick and nauseated. He had unknowingly killed one who was helping stand against the Ice Giants.

"As I was saying, Wigmir has agreed to help us regain the balance of Enceladus," said Dragonwülf.

Wigmir, a towering figure with shimmering icy skin and piercing blue eyes, nodded in agreement. "Wigmir owes you and your crew a debt. Wigmir will not let these criminals harm the colony."

As the ship docked at the colony, Dragonwülf and his crew could see the chaos unfolding outside. Ice giants, much larger and more ferocious than Wigmir, were hurling massive ice boulders at the colony's protective shields. The borders of the city were lined with hundreds of citizens who had been impaled on spikes buried in the snow and ice. Wigmir witnessed the grisly scene before him and barked a painful howl of grief as was never heard from an ice giant.

"We are too late! In the name of the Gods, we are too late. Damn him to hell!" he cried. The renegade ice giants had used the massacre of the innocents to seize power from the weak.

"We must act fast," Dragonwülf said, with urgency in his voice. "Wigmir, it's time to show them what wonders you can do."

With a determined look, Wigmir strode out of the ship, his presence commanding respect and fear. "Stop this madness, you are my brothers and sisters!" he bellowed in a booming voice that echoed across the moon's surface.

The renegade ice giants turned to face Wigmir, their eyes filled with surprise and disbelief. "Wigmir, why do you side with these puny beings?" one of them growled.

"Because they are my friends and Wigmir will not let you harm them or this colony," he declared, his voice unwavering.

Deep within the icy expanse of Saturn's moon, Enceladus, a fierce battle was about to repeat itself. The Deepwater Watchman had returned to the correct time corridor sometime before the cataclysmic attack by the deadly ice giants. Wigmir, the legendary Ice Giant known for his immense power and benevolent nature, stood amidst a group of renegade ice giants who had succumbed to the darkness within their hearts.

"You have strayed from the path of harmony and embraced the shadows," Wigmir's voice echoed across the frozen landscape. "Wigmir cannot allow you to bring chaos and destruction to these lands."

The leader of the renegade ice giants, Frostbite, sneered. "We have grown tired of your preaching, old giant. It is time for a new era to begin, one ruled by strength and power!"

With a roar, the renegade ice giants charged toward Wigmir, their icy claws glinting in the dim light of Saturn. The ice giant braced himself, summoning the ancient powers of frost and ice to aid him in the battle ahead.

The clash of ice against ice filled the air as the two sides collided with a deafening roar. Frostbite and Wigmir locked eyes, their powers of frost and cold swirling around them in a deadly dance.

"Why do you choose this path of destruction, Frost-bite?" The old giant's voice was laced with sadness. "There is still time to turn back."

Frostbite laughed a cruel sound that cut through the frozen air. "It is too late for that, you ragged slush pile. The darkness has consumed us, and there is no turning back now."

As the battle raged on, the landscape of Enceladus trembled under the sheer force of their powers. Ice spikes shot up from the ground, icicles rained down from the sky, and frost-covered boulders were hurled with deadly accuracy.

Amid the chaos, Wigmir and Frostbite continued their intense battle, each refusing to back down. Icy sweat trickled down Wigmir's brow as he poured all of his strength and will into combating the darkness that threatened to engulf them all. Wigmir raised his massive head to the heavens and emitted a piercing howl heard throughout the moon. The shriek shattered ice windows and caused icebergs to crumble. It was a sad and moaning cry for help from old friends.

"Wigmir has called to the sleeping frost giants who slumber in lazy sleep for centuries beneath the surface of the moon.

"You knew these warriors were there all the time?" asked Dragonwülf as the Frost Giants rose to the surface by the hundreds.

"I was not sure I could summon them." He turned his attention to his adversary. "You were once a noble ice giant, Frost-bite," Wigmir said through gritted teeth."

Frostbite's eyes gleamed with madness as he unleashed a devastating blast of icy energy towards Wigmir. With a mighty roar, Wigmir countered the attack, sending a wave of freezing frost back towards Frostbite.

The renegade ice giant screamed in fury as the frost engulfed him, freezing him solidly in a block of ice. The other renegade ice giants looked on in horror as their leader was defeated by the sheer will and power of Wigmir.

Wigmir's voice boomed across the battlefield. "Stop this madness!"

The marching army of the sleeping Frost Giants slogged toward the battlefield as ice fell from them in long sheets, shattering to the ground with each step.

"We have heard the cry of good Wigmir!" bellowed Ice-Whisper, the leader of the sleepers. We are here and ready to do battle with those who would do him and his companions harm!" She stood ready with her soldiers, with their swords at the ready. Prepare to die, Frost-bite!"

"You cannot defeat us, Ice Whisper!" one of the renegades taunted, swinging a massive ice spear toward the ice giant.

She was quicker, summoning a swirling blizzard of ice that engulfed her enemies, freezing them in their tracks.

In the icy expanse of Saturn's moon, a fierce battle was about to unfold. The towering figure of Wigmir, the legendary Ice Giant, stood at the forefront, his ice-blue eyes shining with determination. Surrounding him were a group of loyal ice giants, their breath forming frosty clouds in the frigid air.

"We will not let these renegade ice giants terrorize our home any longer!" declared Wigmir, his voice booming across the icy landscape.

A sinister laugh echoed through the icy canyons as the evil renegade ice giants emerged from the shadows, their eyes glowing with malice. "You have awakened from your slumber just to die," sneered their leader, a hulking figure with jagged icicles protruding from his shoulders. "Prepare to taste defeat."

The two hulking groups charged toward each other, the ground shaking beneath their massive footsteps. Clashes of ice and rock filled the air as the giants collided, their roars echoing through the frozen valleys.

"Stay together, brothers! We fight as one!" shouted Wigmir as he swung his massive ice axe, cleaving through his enemies with precision.

The renegade ice giants fought fiercely, their dark hearts filled with hatred and rage. Wigmir and his loyal companions stood strong, their bond of unity giving them strength in the face of adversity.

"Is that all you can summon?" taunted Wigmir, his eyes blazing with determination.

As the battle raged on, the icy ground became slick with blood and frost. The clash of weapons and the cries of the giants filled the air, creating a symphony of chaos and defiance.

During the chaos, Wigmir faced off against the renegade leader, their weapons clashing with thunderous force. Sparks flew as the two giants exchanged blows, each determined to emerge victorious.

With a mighty roar, Wigmir summoned all his strength and delivered a final, devastating blow, shattering his enemy's icy armor and sending him crashing to the ground.

The evil renegade ice giants, witnessing the fall of their leader, knew they were no match for Wigmir and his loyal companions. With a defeated grumble, they retreated into the shadows, defeated.

As the dust settled and the echoes of battle faded, Wigmir turned to his companions, a proud smile on his face.

"We have defended our home and our honor," he declared. "We are giants of ice, and nothing can break our spirit! Remember, friends, they will return when they regroup. Ice Whisper and all of her ice soldiers will be waiting at the ready to protect our world.

We must now set our sights on freeing the people of the Temple of Enceladus.

The Iron Catacombs

Amidst the icy landscape of Saturn's moon, Enceladus stood the ominous Temple of Enceladus—the heart of darkness that spread fear and despair among the moon's inhabitants. The cold, stoned walls of the temple echoed with the sinister chants of the evil priests who ruled with an iron fist, sacrificing innocent lives to appease their manufactured deity. Jarvis Nightwish once held the position of High Executioner of the Temple. Even the most minor of infractions would result in execution.

As the crew neared the temple gates, the evil priests, clad in dark robes and wielding twisted staffs, emerged to confront the intruders. The rituals for the evening had not begun, so the people of the Temple had not yet arrived.

"Who dares defy the will of the priests of Enceladus?" the high priest sneered, his voice low and full of hate. "Demonstrate the holy hand gestures to gain entrance at once! You should know how to prove yourselves worthy!"

"We are not here to worship you fools," said Dragonwülf. "We are here to put an end to your reign of terror."

Wigmir declared his voice rumbling like thunder. "Your days of sacrificing the innocent are over."

"It is I, Jarvis Nightwish!" he said as he lowered the hood on his temple robe, uncovering his face. "Your time is now! You have hurt and killed your last innocent."

"I knew that you should have faced the disruptor many years ago," said the Priest. "How have you become so pious? There is no larger hypocrite here. You killed on our orders for minor infractions and were happy to do it. The corpses of hundreds lie at your feet! How do you propose to escape that?"

"I have already paid with my life at the hands of The Destiny of Tyr, and I have made amends to the best of my ability," said Nightwish

"No matter, though, step forward and receive the wrath of the gods. You must pay at the temple as well."

A fierce battle ensued, with the clash of steel on steel echoing through the icy corridors of the temple. Wigmir's mighty fists smashed through the ranks of the evil priests, while Jarvis Nightwish moved with deadly precision, his disruptor flashing in the dim torchlight.

"Enough!" bellowed the high priest, his face contorted with rage. "You cannot stop the will of the gods and priests of Enceladus!"

Wigmir and Jarvis fought on, their determination unwavering. With a final, thunderous blow, Wigmir shattered the obsidian altar at the heart of the temple, causing the ground to tremble and crack beneath their feet.

As the temple crumbled around them, the people of Enceladus emerged from their hiding places, their faces filled with hope and gratitude. They looked upon Wigmir and Jarvis as heroes, the saviors who had freed them from the grip of the evil temple.

"The reign of darkness is over," Jarvis proclaimed, his voice filled with triumph. "Enceladus is free once more."

As the battle raged on, the temple itself seemed to rebel against their presence. The walls groaned and shifted, cracks snaking their way across the ancient, stone-like veins of darkness.

"Shake this abomination to the ground!" Dragonwülf shouted, his voice barely audible over the cacophony of destruction. "Nightwish, can you weaken its foundations with your Disruptor?"

He nodded, his brow furrowed in concentration. With a wave of his hand, he summoned a swirling vortex of energy that pulsed with a blinding light. The very ground beneath the temple trembled, and the walls began to crumble like sandcastles before a rising tide.

The trio fought their way to safety as the temple collapsed around them, the oppressive darkness giving way to blinding light as the structure imploded upon itself in a cataclysmic display of destruction.

The Temple of Enceladus was no more, its awful presence erased from the world forever.

Artifact Two

The Shadow of Sarajevo

Dimension of Loki 1914 CE Sarajevo, Bosnia, Assassination of Franz Ferdinand

The man's words echoed through the night, carrying with them a chilling certainty of his intent. The air grew heavy with the weight of his hate, his eyes on fire that burned hotter than the flames.

In the early summer of 1914, when tensions were escalating between nations and the world teetered on the edge of a catastrophic war, a clandestine group called the B*lack Hand* emerged from the shadows. The attention of The Destiny of Tyr was focused with laser intensity on these warmongers and assassins. Much to the dismay of Dragonwülf, the search for the Impaler must wait on larger issues. This mysterious organization had a unique mission: to alter the course of history by preventing the assassination of Archduke Franz Ferdinand. Only The Defiler could control this many people like marionettes on strings.

Deep within the hidden chambers of an ancient castle, the Destiny Council convened. Avat'or, wise and enigmatic, had foreseen the devastating consequences of the Archduke's death. He believed that by preventing the assassination, they could avert the looming horrors of World War I.

"Why is this so important?" asked Luciano Cantore. "I do not understand why one man's death caused such a long and bloody war."

"Very good question, old boy," answered Sir Robert. "I lived through this time. Please allow me to explain. The Prince was next in line for the throne of Austria-Hungary. The Serbians, as expected, refused to let any Austrian officials investigate the assassination of the Prince. In return, Austria declared war on Serbia on July 28, 1914.

Russia was an ally of Serbia and sent its army to defend Serbia.

Germany also declared war on France, Russia's ally, and before long, World War I was underway."

"All for one man?" asked Luciano.

"It does seem that way, my friend, but in truth, Austria started a chain of events after demanding Serbia let them investigate the assassination," added Sir Robert. Even my home, Great Britain, was forced to get involved. It broke my heart to see so many young men die on the battlefield."

Make no mistake, men, the Defiler's filthy hands are all over the Black Hand," declared a determined Dragonwülf.

The council knew Dragonwülf's plan was daring, but they were willing to risk everything to achieve their noble objective.

"Let us bring our best assassins to bear on this plot by the Black Hand. The Defiler will not be victorious!"

"Our dear Dragonwülf, we were not able to stop Abraham from being killed by the Defiler," added one of the Destiny members. "How can we stop this?"

"I will not fail this time! I cannot fail because there is too much at stake. We will bring our entire crew with us, and we will be victorious. I swear on the name of Róthul-Orkr!" said Dragonwülf.

"Thank you for your bravery, Norseman," said Abraham Lincoln politely. "A second chance at life is greatly appreciated. I know you and Mr. Boyd did all that you could to change my life story. You have given me hope where there was none. So you see, you and Mr. Boyd did not fail; you enabled me to continue to change the world for good."

"I can second that," said Viktor Vorobyev.

"This may be more difficult for the crew this time. We believe that the Black Hand has many *deadly fingers* and they will all be along the parade route of the Archduke," said Avat'or.

"We will all be there," said Jarvis Nightwish. "They will be no match for one who has fought the ice giants of Jupiter."

"Aye, my crew will be along the route to kill any man that lifts a finger toward the Archduke," said Captain Old-Turas. "We will just call it pirate justice."

Dragonwülf paused thoughtfully. "I have faced adversaries both on the battlefield and within myself, each obstacle a test of my resolve and determination. The Black Hand will not defeat us."

Lincoln paused thoughtfully for a moment," Through every victory and defeat, I have learned that true honor is not bestowed, but earned through unwavering commitment and unwavering dedication. *Glory* is not found in the spoils of war but in the courage to face adversity head-on and emerge triumphant."

"You see, men, this is why we have Mr. Lincoln with us. Who else can speak so well?"

Weeks before the fateful day in Sarajevo, Dragonwülf deployed his agents across Europe. Each member was paired with a skilled companion, forming an intricate network that spanned the continent. They infiltrated cities, mingled with influential figures, and gathered information crucial to their audacious mission.

Jarvis Nightwish, who was also a master of disguise, assumed the identity of a wealthy Baron. Infiltrating high society in Vienna, he swiftly gained the attention of those close to the Archduke. Jarvis' charisma and quick thinking allowed him to secure an invitation to the royal motorcade's procession through Sarajevo.

Meanwhile, Sir Robert Winterfall devised a plan to disable the engine of the car that would carry the Archduke and his wife, Sophie. He spent days analyzing their itinerary, studying every aspect of the motorcade route, and identifying the perfect location for an intervention.

As the day approached, tension hung heavy in the air. The Dragonwülf and crew were about to alter the course of history and possibly rewrite the fate of nations.

On the morning of June 28, 1914, Jarvis donned a Tuxedo with tails and elegantly boarded the grand motorcade. Within his hidden pockets, he carried a device created by Sir Robert, capable of discreetly disabling any vehicle's engine. As the procession entered Sarajevo's crowded streets, Jarvis's hands trembled with both trepidation and hope. "Do not fear," he told Dragonwülf. "I am still in possession of the greatest close combat weapon in history, the Disruptor."

"We will be in place along the parade route in a very short time. Be ready!" ordered Dragonwülf.

The Black Hand

In a dimly lit warehouse deep within the city, members of the Black Hand gathered around a large wooden table, their faces shrouded in shadows cast by the flickering candles placed in the center. The tension in the room was palpable as they discussed their elaborate plan to assassinate Prince Franz Ferdinand.

"We cannot afford any mistakes in this operation," the leader of the Black Hand, a man known only as Nikola, declared in a commanding tone. "The fate of our cause rests on the success of this mission."

Several gunmen sat around the table as they listened intently to Nikola's instructions. One of them, a burly man with a scar across his cheek, spoke up. "How do you propose we isolate the prince on the parade route without arousing suspicion? If they detect us, we may not get another opportunity.

Nikola paused for a moment before responding. "We have obtained detailed information about the Prince's travel route. He will be passing through the city in an open car on his way to the town hall. We will position our gunmen strategically along the route and strike at the perfect moment. We also have a special bomb made just for this occasion. We cannot miss."

The gunmen nodded in agreement, understanding the gravity of the mission they were about to undertake. Just as they began to finalize their plans, the sound of footsteps echoed in the warehouse, and a young man with piercing eyes entered the room.

"Who is this?" one of the gunmen asked, eyeing the newcomer suspiciously.

Nikola smiled slightly and gestured towards the young man. "This is Gavrilo Princip, our newest recruit. He will be joining us on the mission to eliminate the Prince."

Gavrilo nodded in greeting, his gaze unwavering as he spoke. "I have studied the Prince's movements extensively. I know exactly when and where to strike."

The gunmen exchanged wary glances, unsure of the newcomer's abilities. Nikola placed a reassuring hand on Gavrilo's shoulder and spoke with confidence. "Trust in Gavrilo's expertise. He will not disappoint us."

Dragonwülf and the Prince

Just as the Archduke's car approached the predetermined spot, Jarvis activated the device. Smoke billowed from the engine, causing the vehicle to sputter and come to a halt. Chaos reigned on the streets as a confused and angry crowd gathered.

Alarmed by the sudden turn of events, Archduke Franz Ferdinand and Sophie decided to abandon their plans to visit the wounded who had been injured earlier in the day by the Black Hand. They redirected their motorcade to a safer and less crowded area.

As the Dragonwülf agents observed from a distance, a sense of relief washed over them. It seemed their intervention had succeeded. However, fate had a strange way of ensuring historical events followed their predetermined path.

While the Archduke's car maneuvered through the streets, it made an unexpected wrong turn. In an ironic twist of destiny, fate had intervened.

There, standing frustrated at the side of the road, was Gavrilo Princip, a young Bosnian member of a nationalist group known as the Black Hand.

Seizing the opportunity, Princip pulled out his pistol and fired at the Archduke and his wife, Sophie. The bullets found their mark, and history continued on its predetermined course. The specter of World War I loomed larger than ever before.

As news of the assassination reverberated across the globe, the members of The Destiny of Tyr felt a sense of bitter disappointment. They had fought against the tides of destiny and come up short. Yet, despite their failure, they took solace in the knowledge that they had done everything in their power to prevent the catastrophic war that would consume the world for the next four years.

They returned to the shadows, their existence shrouded in secrecy. The world would never know of their noble attempt to alter history's relentless march. Within their hearts, they held the undying hope that their actions had made a difference, no matter how small.

The events of that early summer in 1914 would forever be etched in the annals of history. The assassination of Archduke Franz Ferdinand changed the world's trajectory, plunging nations into a colossal conflict that cost millions of lives.

Once again, aboard the Deepwater, a frustrated Dragonwülf and his fellowship began to murmur amongst themselves concerning the attempt to save Prince Ferdinand. As Dragonwülf and the crew of the Deepwater Watchman sailed through the endless expanse of space, their somber mood matched the dark void around them. The ship hummed softly as they gathered in the common room, their faces clouded with disappointment and frustration.

"I still cannot believe we could not save Prince Ferdinand," Dragonwülf muttered, his rugged features twisted in a scowl. "It was too quick... too precise. What good is the manipulation of history if we cannot change any of it?"

"It is not the first time we have faced such a challenge," Captain Old-Turas added, his tone grim. "But this time, we were so close..."

As the crew murmured in agreement, Sir Robert sighed deeply." Perhaps time travel was never the solution," he suggested quietly. "Maybe some events are just meant to happen..."

"Damned time travel," grumbled Viktor. "It is an unpredictable thing, always twisting and turning against us. If we dive into a time corridor, we are just taking a chance that it will work in our favor."

Avat'or watched his companions with a calm expression. "Time is a river with many currents," he began, his voice steady and sure. "We must learn to navigate it with grace and acceptance. We can only attempt to bend it to our will. Your efforts were valiant, and that is what matters."

"But we were too late," Dragonwülf argued, his eyes flashing with frustration. "What good are our skills and traveling the corridors of time if we can't change the course of destiny?"

"Time is not promised, my friends," Nightwish spoke. "We may not have saved Prince Ferdinand this time, but who is to say our actions won't change something important through the fabric of time and bring about a different outcome in the future?"

Avat'or smiled gently. "Nightwish is correct. Time is not linear; it is a tapestry of possibilities. Our actions, no matter how small, can have far-reaching consequences that we may not see immediately. "Prince Ferdinand's legacy lives on, and our actions have not been in vain."

The crew fell silent, pondering Avat'or's words. In their doubts and sorrows, his wisdom offered a glimmer of hope and understanding.

The clipper ship ventured forth, a beacon of light in the darkness of space, its crew united in purpose and determination.

The Defiler remained two steps ahead of the Deepwater Watchman.

Artifact Three

The Lords of the Trenches

herranna dróttnar

Dimension of Loki 1914-1919 CE

World War 1 No Man's Land

Through the corridors of time, I have witnessed the depths of depravity that mortals are capable of, their hearts corrupted by greed and their spirits consumed by hatred.

The Tale of Dragonwülf and Secret Treaties

As news of the assassination spread, it sent shockwaves throughout Europe and beyond. The political landscape was already tense, with rivalries and alliances brewing beneath the surface. The assassination of Prince Ferdinand only served to ignite the powder keg that was waiting to explode.

In the halls of power, leaders scrambled to make sense of the events unfolding in Sarajevo. The assassination of a royal heir was an act of aggression that could not go unanswered. As tensions rose, diplomatic channels were put to the test, with ultimatums and threats being exchanged between nations.

One such conversation took place between the leaders of Austria-Hungary and Germany:

"We cannot let this act go unpunished," the Austrian-Hungarian Emperor declared.

"I agree, but we must tread carefully. The repercussions of a hasty response could be catastrophic," the German Emperor replied.

As the days turned into weeks, the world held its breath, waiting to see how the great powers would respond to the assassination of Prince Ferdinand. In the end, a series of alliances and secret treaties would ultimately draw the world into the chaos of war.

On July 28, 1914, Austria-Hungary declared war on Serbia, setting off a chain reaction of declarations and mobilizations. In the blink of an eye,

Europe was plunged into the horrors of World War I, a conflict that would claim millions of lives and reshape the world forever.

Gavrilo Princip sat in his prison cell, a small smile playing on his lips. He had achieved his goal, albeit at a great cost. The assassination of Prince Ferdinand had indeed been the catalyst that threw the world into chaos, changing the course of history in ways no one could have imagined.

The fields of Europe, once filled with green grass, cattle, and beauty, were now filled with foxholes, barbed wire, and the stench of mustard gas.

One foggy morning, the crew of the Deepwater Watchman found themselves above a WWI battlefield, the smell of gunpowder lingering in the air. Captain Old-Turas stroked his beard thoughtfully as he gazed down at the chaos below.

"We can't just ignore this, lads," he declared, his voice gruff but determined. "We have the power to make a difference here. Dragonwülf, are you up for the task?"

"You ask an ancient warrior if he is ready for war. Are you daft, you salty old fool?" answered Dragonwülf, laughing. We know that the Defiler is the cause of the abomination that rages below."

"He is most likely a General or other high-ranking officer," added Old-Turas.

"Let me go down there. I'll find him and put a slug in his pumpkin for him," said Luciano Cantore.

"Nay, this is a task for one seasoned in the throes of battle," said Dragonwülf.

"We're both pretty good at killin' guys that need killin'," said Viktor. "Luciano and I got this!"

"Your time will come, comrades," answered Dragonwülf. There will be a time in the panorama of history where your bullets will be required, but not yet."

As he prepared to be lowered onto the battlefield below, the crew gathered around him, offering words of encouragement and support.

"Remember, Dragonwülf, you do not have the speed or the agility to navigate this dangerous terrain," said Sir Robert, his brown eyes filled with concern. "We must remember our age, good Ser."

Dragonwülf smiled reassuringly. "I will not fail; I will do whatever it takes to find the Defiler in this hellish place.

The council of The Destiny of Tyr was in array aboard the Deepwater Watchman, along with new member President Abraham Lincoln.

"Welcome, Mr. President, said Avat'or. We are in anxious anticipation of your wisdom for the mission ahead. As you know, we were unable to save Prince Ferdinand from the assassin's bullet. What we have learned from this encounter with history is that some shadows of the past are simply meant to be."

"How did you arrive at this?" asked Lincoln.

Avat'or answered pensively, "We disabled the Prince's automobile, hoping to save him from the gauntlet that lay before him, and it just placed him in the line of fire anyway. We are greatly disappointed. We feel that the assassin was indeed The Defiler, disguised as a Serbian national."

Lincoln sighed and then made a sobering statement. "I do understand your disappointment, my friend. I was unable to stop the War Between the States, no matter what I did."

Unfortunately, the world is in the throes of a deadly war for which there seems to be no end," said Dragonwülf. "The death of Prince Ferdinand set the war in motion."

"I thought I would never again see the day when my brother fought so horribly against my brother in another wasteful and useless war. It is brother against brother, father against son, one bloody year after another. I prayed I would never again see this, but it was not to be. My dear God in heaven's ear remained deaf to my pleas. It is almost too great for my heart to bear. I feel it breaking in my poor old chest. This must end, and it must never happen again. I left many friends and comrades back on the battlefield of Antietam and Wilson's Creek. The battles of this bloody war are no exception. My old heart will be buried in both places along with my friends from long ago," lamented the President.

With a whoosh of steam and a jolt, Dragonwülf rode on the back of Morning Fire down to the battlefield, the sounds of cannons and gunfire growing louder with each passing second. He hid her giant form in the forest adjacent to the battlefield.

"Stay here, fierce one, until I call for you," said Dragonwülf.

"I will be here for you as always," said Morning Fire.

He took a deep breath and surveyed the scene before him. The British Soldiers were locked in a fierce battle, their faces etched with fear and determination.

"Hello, lads!" Dragonwülf called out, his voice carrying over the chaotic noise.

The soldiers paused, their eyes widening in disbelief at the sight of this strange figure in a black suit standing before them.

"Who are you?" one of them asked, his gun still raised but his grip loosening.

"My name is…Wolf. I am here to fight alongside you in this battle of righteousness."

"Who told you this war had anything to do with righteousness?" asked a young soldier. "Are you daft?"

The air was thick with the stench of mud and gunpowder, while the distant echoes of artillery fire filled the horizon. Among them was Lieutenant Thomas Sullivan, a seasoned officer with a weathered face and hardened eyes."

Private Wolf! Grab a rifle and fall in with the rest of your platoon!" ordered Lt. Sullivan. "Your beard is not a regulation beard, soldier! That thing must be two years old. How were you allowed to grow this?"

"I have been away," answered Dragonwülf.

As the sun began to rise, casting a fiery glow over the battlefield, Lieutenant Sullivan gathered his troops around him. "Men, today we face our greatest challenge yet. The enemy is close, and they will stop at nothing to break our lines. However, we will not falter. We will stand tall and fight with every ounce of courage in our hearts!"

His words stirred something deep within the soldiers, reigniting the flames of patriotism and determination. Private Tipsworth, a young soldier with a nervous disposition, spoke up, "But, Sir, how can we hope to hold the line against such overwhelming odds?"

Lieutenant Sullivan turned to face him, his gaze unwavering. "We may be outnumbered, but we have something they don't. We have each other. We have the bonds of unity forged in the fires of battle. And as long as we stand together, we are invincible."

Just then, the sound of distant footsteps and clanking metal broke through the eerie silence, signaling the approach of the enemy. The soldiers readied their rifles, their hearts pounding in unison as they awaited the impending storm.

As the first wave of enemy soldiers emerged from the fog, a hail of bullets erupted from both sides, filling the air with a deafening roar. The battlefield was engulfed in chaos, the symphony of war unfolding before their eyes. Men cried out in pain, the earth trembled beneath their feet, and the sky seemed to weep tears of blood.

As the battle raged on, Dragonwülf's presence on the battlefield sparked a mix of fear and awe among the soldiers. His sword gleamed with an otherworldly light as he charged into the fray.

"Who is that?" one soldier whispered to his comrade as they watched Dragonwülf cleave through enemy lines with unmatched skill.

Amidst the chaos, Lieutenant Sullivan's voice rang out like a beacon of hope. "Hold the line, men! Stand firm and fight with all your might!" His words were met with a chorus of battle cries as the soldiers rallied around him, pushing back against the relentless tide of enemy forces.

For hours on end, the battle raged on, the fate of the battalion being uncertain. Each man fought with a courage born of desperation, their spirits unbroken despite the overwhelming odds. The enemy forces began to overwhelm the British soldiers, and all looked like it might be lost. Dragonwülf stood defiant above the foxholes and cried out with a loud voice. "Come to me, Morning Fire of the Sky!"

"The other soldiers were transfixed on the bravery or foolishness of this bearded soldier from another land.

The sky was filled with smoke and screams, the ground trembling with the force of artillery. In the chaos stood a group of weary soldiers, their faces etched with fear and exhaustion as they fought through the muddy trenches of the Western Front during World War I.

"Keep moving, lads! *We will hold* this position at all costs!" ordered Lt. Sullivan.

A Private with a shaky voice looked up at the officer with wide eyes. "Sir, what are we going to do? We're outnumbered and outgunned!"

Lt. Sullivan clenched his jaw, his mind racing for a plan. "We need a miracle, lads. We need something to turn the tide in our favor."

"Come to me, Morning Fire of the Sky!" rang out through the battlefield over the trenches.

Suddenly, a deafening roar echoed through the battlefield, causing both the Allied and enemy troops to pause in their tracks. A massive shadow fell over the soldiers as a dragon, its scales shimmering in the sunlight, soared overhead with majestic wings.

Private Tipsworth gasped in awe. "By the heavens, what is that?"

Lt. Sullivan watched in disbelief as the dragon swooped down, breathing fire upon the enemy lines and scattering them in a panic. "It is a bloody dragon! I cannot believe my eyes! Perhaps it is a dream.

The dragon landed gracefully in front of the group of soldiers, its eyes shining with intelligence and compassion. "Fear not, brave humans. I am here to help you in your time of need."

Private Tipsworth stumbled forward, his voice filled with wonder and trembling, "Thank you, noble creature! You have saved us from certain death!"

"Private Wolf! Do you have anything to do with this? What do you know?" asked the Officer.

"Yes, brave soldier. She is my dragon, given to me by those who wish to stop this war. If I told you anymore, you would not believe me."

Dragonwülf climbed upon the back of the Morning Fire and flew into the darkened sky. As the dragon lifted off once more, the soldiers watched in silence, their hearts filled with newfound courage and determination. For on that day, they had witnessed a miracle – a dragon coming to their rescue amid the horrors of war, reminding them that even during darkness, there is always light to be found. The German foxhole lit up with rifle and mortar fire as the dragon lifted into the sky. Just as Dragonwülf was being carried out of sight, a shell exploded, throwing Dragonwülf to the ground from high atop the dragon's back. His wounded body fell into the field below as Morning Fire climbed to get away from the crossfire.

Finally, as the sun began to set on the horizon, the enemy forces began to waver. The symphony of war had reached its crescendo, with victory within reach. Lieutenant Sullivan raised his sword high in the air, a beacon of triumph amidst the smoke and chaos.

In the devastation of the battle, a young British officer named John found himself separated from his unit after the brutal battle. Lost and disoriented, he stumbled upon the wounded Dragonwülf lying in a secluded foxhole surrounded by mud, blood, and the bodies of soldiers. The warrior's armor was weathered and covered in symbols unknown to John. His eyes held the wisdom of centuries past.

"My name is Dragonwülf," the ancient warrior rasped as John approached cautiously. "I fought in battles long forgotten, and now I find myself wounded and alone."

Moved by compassion, John immediately set to work tending to Dragonwülf's injuries, using whatever supplies he had at his disposal. As John nursed Dragonwülf back to health, the old warrior began to recount tales of his adventures and battles from a time when legends roamed the earth.

"Did you not fear death?" John asked. You came very close a few times."

"No, I do not, nor have I ever, feared death. I often fear the enemy and his weapons of pain, but I do not fear death," said Dragonwülf. "We never leave the fellowship of our loved ones or comrades when we taste death. We just melt into a mist alongside the present realm. We breathe deeply in death just beyond the reach of the living world, on the other side of the new morning. We rise with the day and sleep with the night; all the while, we watch and wait. Have no fear, they are with us always."

With each passing day, John listened intently to Dragonwülf's stories, marveling at the bravery and valor displayed by the ancient warrior. Dragonwülf spoke of epic quests, mythical creatures, and ancient kingdoms lost to the annals of time. John was captivated by the tales, feeling a deep connection to the warrior and his experiences.

"My life has become a struggle for existence. I find it a chore to rise each day and fight a new fight. Do not mistake me; I am not a coward in any way. I am just weary to the bone with the futility of it all," said John. "To exist is the task."

"Life is not merely about existence, but about the pursuit of honor, glory, and victory. Each day, I rise with a fire in my heart, driven by a relentless desire to conquer challenges and emerge victorious. The battles I have fought, wars I have waged, all in the name of upholding honor and achieving glory. For what is life without honor?"

"I have honor, and I believe there are times when war is necessary, but the thought of the enemy bearing down upon us sometimes is too great," said John."

"The sound of marching feet is like a dagger to my soul, my friend. It tears and pierces the flesh of my spirit and brings me to my knees. There is neither balm nor bandage that can heal me from the wounds of war. I am left with scars that never heal. So is a Hrothgorn likened unto *your* enemies."

Inspired by Dragonwülf's stories, John began to weave his own tales, drawing from the ancient warrior's words and creating a rich tapestry of myths and legends. He spent hours writing and scribbling in his journal, giving life to characters and lands born from the depths of Dragonwülf's memories.

As the days turned into weeks, the young officer, Lt. John Ronald Reuel Tolkien's journal was filled with stories of a dark lord who sought to enslave the world. He poured his heart and soul into his writing, creating a tale of epic proportions.

When Dragonwülf finally regained his strength and bid John farewell, the young officer knew that he had been forever changed by the warrior's presence. The most important thing Dragonwülf was able to learn from this young officer was the name of a German General whom the men nicknamed "Der Dämon." His men were terrified of his very presence.

Artifact Four

General Hans Von Huberdorf

Dimension of Óðinn (1943 CE)

Verluste sind mir egal.
"Alles, was zählt, ist der Sieg um jeden Preis."
General Hans Von Huberdorf.

"Casualties are of no concern to me.
All that matters is victory at any cost."

General Hans Von Huberdorf was a name whispered with fear by both friend and foe alike on the battlefield of World War I. Tall and imposing, with a stern face and piercing blue eyes, he was a strategic mastermind whose brilliance knew no bounds.

One cold and misty morning, as the sounds of cannon fire echoed across the barren landscape, General Huberdorf stood surveying the battlefield from a small mound. Beside him, his trusted Lieutenant, Karl, waited for orders.

"Karl, we are facing a formidable enemy today," the General stated calmly, his voice carrying authority born of years of experience. "But we shall emerge victorious."

Karl nodded his admiration for his commanding officer, evident in his eyes. "What are your orders, Herr General?"

"We shall employ a tactic that the enemy never sees coming," General Huberdorf replied, a sly smile playing on his lips. "We shall feign weakness in the north, drawing their forces towards us. Meanwhile, our main attack will come from the south, where we shall catch them unawares."

"A diversionary tactic! Herr General, that is brilliant!" said his officer.

With a nod, General Huberdorf turned to his assembled troops. "Men, today we make history. Today, we show the world the might of the German army! The screaming trenches of death keep dark secrets. Those who survive this torture no longer have voices. The screams have ruined their throats with raw fury like torn fingernails on the inside of a coffin," he said with a demonic grin that terrified Karl.

As the battle raged on, the enemy fell into the trap laid out by General Huberdorf. Chaos ensued as the German forces struck with precision and ferocity, overwhelming their foes at every turn.

In the aftermath of the battle, General Huberdorf and Lieutenant Karl stood amidst the carnage, victorious but somber.

"Well done, Karl," the General said, clapping his lieutenant on the shoulder. "Your bravery and quick thinking were instrumental in our victory today."

Karl beamed with pride, knowing that he had earned the respect of his esteemed commander. As Karl looked upon his commanding officer, for a brief flash, he saw a countenance of bloody fangs and searing eyes. He beheld the bloody and grotesque face of Orgo the Impaler.

"Oh, my Holy Lord! What have you become, Herr General?" screamed Karl as his entire body began to quiver.

"Speak nothing of what you have seen today! Do you understand?" said the General in a threatening tone.

"Yes, Herr General, I have seen nothing today," answered a shaken Karl.

As they began the long trudge back to their camp, General Huberdorf paused, gazing out across the battlefield. "War is a terrible thing, Karl. However, sometimes, it is unavoidable. Remember that."

With those words, General Hans Von Huberdorf, the master strategist of World War I, pulled his pistol from his sidearm belt and shot Lieutenant Karl in the head at direct range. After announcing the Lieutenant's unfortunate death from a sniper, he led his troops back to camp, their heads held high in victory and their hearts heavy with the weight of war.

—————————

The dark clouds loomed over the battlefield as General Hans Von Huberdorf paced back and forth in his tent, his face etched with a sinister grin. The other officers gathered around him, whispering among themselves as they awaited his next command.

"We must strike at dawn," General Huberdorf announced, his voice cold and commanding. "Our enemies will not know what hit them."

"But, Herr General, the enemy is heavily fortified," one officer spoke up hesitantly. "We may suffer heavy casualties if we attack head-on."

General Huberdorf turned to face the officer, his eyes flashing with disdain. "Casualties are of no concern to me," he hissed. "All that matters is victory at any cost."

The officers exchanged uneasy glances, but none dared to challenge the General's orders. They knew all too well the consequences of defying him.

As the night wore on, General Huberdorf meticulously laid out his battle plans, each one more diabolical than the last. His strategies were ruthless and cunning, designed to crush the enemy without mercy.

"The enemy will expect us to attack from the east," General Huberdorf explained, his voice low and menacing. "But we shall strike from the west, catching them off guard and decimating their forces."

The officers nodded in reluctant agreement, still uneasy about the General's lack of effective tactics. However, they knew they had no choice but to follow his lead.

At the rise of the morning sun, the artillery began to fire, signaling the start of the attack. The battlefield erupted into chaos as soldiers charged forward, their cries of battle mingling with the sounds of gunfire and explosions.

General Huberdorf watched from a safe distance, a cruel smile playing on his lips as he witnessed the devastation unfolding before him. His plan was working flawlessly, and victory was within his grasp.

As the day wore on, it became clear that the cost of victory was high. The casualties mounted on both sides, leaving a trail of death and destruction in their wake.

One officer approached General Huberdorf, his face pale with horror. "Sir, we cannot continue like this," he pleaded. "We are losing too many men."

General Huberdorf's eyes narrowed, and his gaze was icy cold. "The cost of victory is always high," he replied. "But it is a price worth paying for glory and conquest."

The officer recoiled, his heart heavy with dread. He knew then that General Huberdorf's lust for power knew no bounds, and that they were all pawns in his twisted game of war.

The battle raged on, with General Hans Von Huberdorf's legacy forever tarnished by the bloodshed Orgo the Impaler unleashed upon the world. A ruthless and cunning general, his name would go down in history as a symbol of evil and tyranny, a cautionary tale of the darkness that lurks within the hearts of men. The war would certainly be shortened if it were not for the ruthless tactics of The Impaler posing as General Von Huberdorf.

The Deepwater Watchman orbited far above the Earth in the realm of the Great War. She had just delivered Jarvis Nightwish to the city of Paris.

General Hans Von Huberdorf found himself embroiled in a covert conspiracy that would forever alter the course of history. Unbeknownst to him, a shadowy figure lurked in the shadows, biding his time, waiting for the perfect moment to strike.

It was on a chilly evening in the heart of Paris, as General Huberdorf retired to his quarters after a long day of planning and strategizing, that the fateful encounter took place. Jarvis Nightwish, a mysterious man rumored to hail from the moon of Saturn and possessing otherworldly powers, materialized out of thin air in the general's chambers, holding a strange and ominous weapon known as the Disruptor.

"Who are you?" General Huberdorf demanded, his hand instinctively reaching for the pistol holstered at his side. However, before he could react,

Jarvis Nightwish raised the Disruptor, its humming energy crackling with an eerie light.

"Do not call for your guards. You will be dead before the words escape you! I am Jarvis Nightwish, from the realms of time," the stranger declared, his voice echoing with a chilling certainty. "And your time has come, General, or should I call you Ogor the Impaler?"

General Huberdorf's eyes widened in disbelief as he beheld the weapon aimed at him, recognizing the dire threat it posed. "What treachery is this? What do you seek to achieve by assassinating me, a soldier sworn to serve his country with honor? Who is Ogor the Impaler? You have me confused with another person, young man!"

"Do not attempt to sway me with your false tongue, Impaler!" said Jarvis.

Nightwish's expression remained impassive, his gaze unfaltering. "Your actions have consequences, Ogor, but you already knew that because the universe is in chaos because of you. The blood you have spilled, the lives you have extinguished... they cry out for justice. And now, you shall face the consequences of your deeds."

With a swift motion, Nightwish touched the shoulder of the Impaler with the Disruptor, unleashing a blinding burst of energy that enveloped General Huberdorf in a blazing inferno. The air filled with the acrid scent of burnt flesh as the once-mighty general was reduced to ashes, his legacy and ambitions consumed by the flames of fate. The spirit of The Impaler arose from the ashes and laughed as it rose through the ceiling of the General's quarters.

"Fool! All you have done is kill a weak-minded idiot, General. You cannot destroy me! Tell the Destiny of Tyr that they must do better than this," said Ogor as he rose into the sky above, abandoning his efforts in World War 1.

As the smoke cleared, Jarvis Nightwish stood alone in the chamber, the Disruptor shimmering with malevolent energy.

General Hans Von Huberdorf met his end at the hands of an executioner from the outer realms of time. Ogor the Impaler and The Defiler of Souls were once again flung into the Panorama and the realms of time. The Great War would come to a grinding halt without the leadership of the General of the German army. Countless lives were saved in this realm.

Artifact Five

The Pirate and the Witch Queen

sjóræninginn ok seiðdrottningin

Dimension of Óðinn (125 AD)
Caribbean Sea/Pirate Realm

"I intend to walk over as much dirt and sand as I am able. I intend to do it before all the dirt and sand walk over me."-
-Old-Turas

Captain Turas stood behind the wheel of the Deepwater Watchman and closed his eyes from exhaustion. He sat softly in his chair behind the great wheel of the ship. His old spirit wandered through the halls of time as he fell fast asleep and dreamed of scanning the turbulent waters for any sign of the dreaded Jörmungandr. His dream crew bustled around him, preparing the cannons and securing the rigging in anticipation of the imminent battle.

"I have heard tales of the Jörmungandr's immense size and strength," one of the crewmembers remarked nervously. "Do you think we stand a chance against such a formidable foe, Captain?"

Turas turned to face the crewmember, his eyes filled with determination. "Fear not, my friends. We may be facing a fearsome enemy, but we are sailors of the sea, and the sea flows in our blood. We will not go down without a fight."

Just then, a massive serpent emerged from the depths, wrapping itself around the mast of the ship. The crew gasped in horror as the Jörmungandr's massive form rose from the water, hissing a horrible spray of seawater.

"Steady, men!" Turas shouted, his voice ringing out across the deck. "Prepare to fire the cannons on my mark!"

The crew sprang into action, operated the cannons, and took aim at the monstrous creature that loomed over them. Turas gripped the wheel tightly, his jaw set in determination.

"Now!" he cried, and the cannons roared to life, sending a barrage of cannonballs hurtling towards the Jörmungandr.

The creature let out a deafening roar of pain as the cannonballs struck true, causing it to thrash wildly in the water. Captain Turas was not done yet. He steered the Silver Serpent closer to Jörmungandr's eye.

"We need to aim for its weak spot!" he shouted to his crew. "Target the eye of the beast!"

The crew followed his command, adjusting their aim to target Jörmungandr's massive eye. With a final volley of cannon fire, the Jörmungandr let out a terrible wail before sinking beneath the waves, defeated at last.

As the crew cheered and celebrated their hard-won victory, Captain Turas stood at the helm, a satisfied smile on his face. "We have faced the Jörmungandr and emerged victorious," he declared. "Let this day be remembered as a testament to the courage and skill of the sailors of the North Hundren."

His dream ship, the North Hundren, sailed on, its crew forever bound by the bonds forged in the heat of battle and the triumph of the indomitable human spirit.

The corridors of memory are a lonely walking distance back to reality. The Captain was, of course, only dreaming of his battle with the Jörmungandr. The Hundren had long lain on the floor of the sea with a broken spine. The Deepwater Watchman was now his ship, and the fate of the world was at stake. He was startled awake by Dragonwülf.

"Captain, are you sleeping?"

"Hell no, I was spending time in prayer to Róthul-Orkr," answered Old Turas.

"I know you better than that."

"I was thinking about the men of my precious North Hundren," answered Turas. When will it be my time to reconcile my timeline and put my universe in balance?"

Dragonwülf answered with a concerned look, "Your time will come."

"Darkness may consume my soul, but it is the world that shall drown in its depths, for when the night falls, and the shadows whisper my name, revenge shall be mine."

"Did you just think of that?" asked Dragonwülf. "It is very poetic."

"Do not make light of my pain! Witch Queen Ingegärd will pay for the destruction of my ship. Her creation, the battle worm Ghidorwrath, destroyed the Hundren as if she were made of balsa wood! When is my time?" he demanded.

"The Witch must make herself known to us. We cannot seek her because her domain is in the spirit realm. I know you know this, Captain," said Dragonwülf.

"I know she resides on the sea. I will have her today. I swear it on your grave and mine!" promised the Captain.

"How do you expect to find her in this darkness?" asked Dr. Winterfall.

"The stars weep for the fallen, the moon mourns the lost. But I embrace the darkness, for it is my only friend," answered Old Turas

"Darkness might be good for you, but we should wait until morning," said Luciano Cantore. "After all, we gotta see what we're doing."

Turas stood at the wheel of The Deep Water Watchman, his gaze fixed on the horizon. The salty wind whipped through his hair, carrying with it a sense of anticipation and dread.

"I know of an incantation that might draw out the Witch," admitted Hansel Gru'el, The Harvester of Eyes, breaking the dark silence.

"This is not the time to draw evil into our midst, Harvester. We must be prepared first," warned Dragonwülf.

Old Turas pulled his side gagger from his sheath. "Now is the time, old Norseman! I will wait no longer for my revenge."

Captain Old Turas stood facing the ancient warrior Dragonwülf in the dimly lit chamber. The two warriors locked eyes, their gazes filled with determination and the promise of a fierce battle. Dragonwülf's ancient sword gleamed in the flickering torchlight, while Captain Turas gripped his dagger tightly, ready for the fight that lay ahead.

"You dare challenge me, Captain Turas?" Dragonwülf's voice boomed through the chamber, echoing off the stoned walls.

"I do," the Captain replied, his voice steady despite the adrenaline coursing through his veins. "I will not let you bring destruction upon this land."

Dragonwülf let out a menacing laugh as he raised his sword, the blade shimmering with otherworldly power. "You cannot hope to defeat me, mortal. I have fought battles that would make your blood run cold."

With a swift movement, Dragonwülf charged toward Captain Turas, swinging his sword in a deadly arc. Turas dodged to the side, narrowly avoiding the blade as he countered with a series of quick strikes from his dagger. The two warriors clashed, the sound of metal ringing out through the chamber as they fought with skill and precision.

"You fight well, Captain," Dragonwülf grunted, his eyes narrowing in concentration. "You are no match for the power that I wield."

Captain Turas gritted his teeth, pushing himself to match Dragonwülf blow for blow. The ancient warrior's strength was formidable, but Turas refused to back down. With a fierce battle cry, he pressed forward, his dagger flashing in the torchlight as he sought an opening.

The old pirates circled each other, their movements a deadly dance of steel and skill. Captain Turas could feel the weight of the battle pressing down on him, but he refused to yield. With a burst of energy, he launched himself at Dragonwülf, his dagger flashing towards the ancient warrior's heart.

Dragonwülf was prepared. With a deft move, he knocked Turas's dagger aside and struck out with his sword, the blade cutting through the air with deadly precision. Turas felt a searing pain in his side as the sword sliced through his armor, drawing blood.

"Enough of this infernal saber rattling!" yelled Dr. Winterfall. "We have too many obstacles to overcome without trying to kill each other. Stop this at once!"

The two adversaries were drawn back to reality and holstered their weapons because they knew what the Professor said was true.

"Gru'el, can you summon the Witch Queen?" asked Dragonwülf.

"I can try to form an incantation," announced Gru'el as he fell to his knees.

"Hear my voice, all ye in the underworld of time. I call upon you to endow me with all knowledge of this witch!" Gru'el's mouth began to form words of an unfamiliar language unknown to the crew."

Per te oculi tui I cognoscente tua secreta et mendacia," (through your eyes I will know your secrets and lies).

His voice became that of the Witch. The voice started as a low, craggy voice and built in intensity.

"Dragonwülf, I see where you lurk. You are near my island and my realm. I curse you and your Destiny of Tyr. I gave your enemies the Portal of the Pines, where they might receive modern weapons to defeat you," hissed the Witch.

The Hrothgorn fought like cowards and lost. You will never defeat me. Your Captain has given you away. The flames of revenge burn brighter than any magic, consuming all in their path. I can see your ship from here. I...will come to you."

Suddenly, a dark shadow fell over the deck, and the Witch Queen materialized before him in a cloud of smoke and shadow.

"Turas, Captain of the Watchman." The Witch's voice was cold and menacing, sending shivers down his spine. "I see you've come seeking revenge for the North Hundren. How predictable."

Turas clenched his fists, his eyes blazing with anger. "You destroyed my ship and killed my crew!" he bellowed. "I will not rest until I have my vengeance."

The Witch Queen chuckled darkly, her eyes glowing with malevolence.

"Oh, but you have forgotten, Captain. I am no ordinary foe. Your petty vengeance means nothing to me."

As she spoke, Gru'el stepped forward, a wicked glint in his gaze. With a swift motion, he reached out and plucked one of the Witch Queen's eyes from its socket, causing her to shriek in pain. The sound echoed across the waves.

"You dare to defy me," the Harvester of Eyes sneered, holding up the eye for all to see. "I shall read your mind and reveal your dark intentions to all." The Harvester of Eyes then inserted her eyeball into his empty eye socket.

The Witch Queen writhed in agony as the Harvester of Eyes delved into her thoughts, his face contorted with concentration. Suddenly, he recoiled, a look of shock crossing his features.

"Evil queen," he whispered, his voice filled with disbelief. "You seek to unleash a great darkness upon the world, a darkness that will consume all in its path."

The crew of the Watchman gasped in horror as the Harvester of Eyes revealed the Witch Queen's plans. Turas felt a chill run down his spine, realizing the true extent of the danger they faced. Her remaining eye was milky white, nearly blinded by the Hansel Gru'el.

"You blind me and then challenge me?" the Witch's voice echoed eerily through the fog.

Captain Turas drew his own sword, his jaw set in determination. "We will not cower before you, sea hag. Your reign of terror ends here."

With a flick of her wrist, the Witch Queen summoned a horde of shadowy creatures to swarm the deck. The crew of the Deepwater Watchman fought valiantly, their swords clashing against the dark magic of their foes. Arrows whistled through the air, finding their marks with deadly accuracy.

Jarvis Nightwish vaulted over a group of creatures, his Disruptor flashing in the dim light. "Get me close to her! All I need to do is touch her with this!"

The battle raged on, the air thick with the smell of blood and magic. The Witch Queen's powers grew stronger with each passing moment, her spells testing the resolve of the crew. Old Captain Turas refused to back down, rallying his sailors with fierce determination.

As the moon rose high in the sky, the tide of the battle turned. With a mighty roar, the Captain and Dragonwülf charged toward the Witch Queen, their swords clashing in a shower of sparks. The crew of the Deepwater Watchman fought with renewed vigor, their loyalty to their captain unbreakable.

In a final, desperate move, the Witch Queen unleashed a wave of pure darkness towards the ship. Before it could reach its target, the Harvester stepped forward, his sword glowing with a brilliant light. With a powerful strike, he shattered the dark wave, sending shards of magic scattering into the night.

The Hag howled in rage, her powers waning as the crew closed in around her. With a defiant cry, Captain Turas plunged his sword into her chest, the blade glowing with a fierce light. Nightwish stepped into the fray and touched the vile witch with the powerful disruptor. She let out a final, chilling scream before crumbling to dust at their feet.

With a final taunting smile, the Witch Queen vanished, leaving the crew of the Watchman to ponder their next move in the face of an impending catastrophe.

"I will go on ahead and clear the way. Our next task is not set before us. I can travel faster on the back of Morning Fire than we can onboard the Deepwater," promised Dragonwülf. "I will await our reunion."

Artifact Six

JYR'DIL
THE LAST STAND OF OGOR

síðasta staða ógs

ᛊᛁᚦᚨᛊᛏᚨ ᛊᛏᚨᚦᚨ ᛟᚷᛊ

Date: Dimension of Óðinn (126 CE)

"Great Tyr, hear our plea. Grant us the strength to face our enemies and emerge victorious in the battles that lie ahead."

In the vast expanse of space, there existed a planet known as Jyr'dil, a world teeming with life and inhabited by humanoid beings. Their peaceful existence was about to be disrupted by The Defiler.

Commanding the Götterdämmerung, he sought to unleash Ogor the Impaler upon the unsuspecting inhabitants of this peaceful planet.

As the Defiler's ship descended upon the tranquil land, a dark shadow loomed over the land, striking fear into the hearts of the beings below. The ship's massive metal hull creaked and groaned as it landed with a resounding thud, signaling the beginning of a nightmare for the inhabitants of Jyr'dil.

From the bowels of the Götterdämmerung emerged Ogor, a creature of immense size and power, have face gleaming with an evil light. His eyes glowed with an otherworldly fire as his voice unleashed a deafening and belching roar that shook the very ground beneath its feet.

"Behold the might of Ogor, The Evil One!" The Defiler's voice echoed across the land through the external sound system, causing panic and despair among the populace. "You shall serve as food for Ogor, and your souls will fuel his eternal hunger!"

"I will take no rest until I see your people perched atop jagged pikes screaming for mercy!" the Impaler said with a sick grin.

"You must excuse the Impaler's enthusiasm; he really puts his heart into his work," said The Defiler. His zeal for victory does save me a large amount of effort in the grand scheme of things."

Amidst the chaos and confusion, a brave group of Jyr'dilian warriors stepped forward to confront the intruder. Their leader, a valiant warrior named Lyra, raised her sword defiantly and called out to The Defiler.

"You will not have our souls, foul creatures!" Lyra's voice rang out with determination but quivered with actual fear. "We will stand against you and protect our home from whatever evil awaits us."

The Defiler's foot soldiers, armed with broad swords and axes, exited the Götterdämmerung from her port side. The two small armies clashed steel upon steel and bone upon bone. The Jyr'dilian warriors were no match for the evil ghouls of the Defiler and the remnants of Caligulis Gulag. The Jyr'dilian warriors fell like wheat against the thresher.

The Defiler sneered, his gaze filled with violent intent as he regarded the warriors before him. "Fools!" he hissed mockingly. "You cannot hope to defeat the power of my creation, Ogor. Surrender now, or face annihilation and be devoured!"

Nearing the planet of Jyr'dil, Dragonwülf rode swiftly atop Morning Fire of the Sky. Together, they soared through the clouds in pursuit of The Defiler.

Witnessing the imminent danger knew that he and Morning Fire must confront this fearsome beast to safeguard Jyr'dil.

As they approached the planet, his eyes filled with fire and power. Ride to the surface he called out to his dragon, his voice ringing with authority and determination.

Ogor reached down, seized the mighty Jyr'dilian warrior Lyra by the throat, and held her high above his open maw.

"Today, this little one will make a magnificent noonday snack!

"Beast of the abyss, you have trespassed upon the sacred lands of Jyr'dil. Unhand her at once, fiend! Prepare to face the wrath of Dragonwülf and Morning Fire of the Sky!" bellowed the old warrior.

Ogor roared in response threw Lyra to the ground, a deafening sound that shook the earth beneath them. He unleashed torrents of fire and ice, his attacks relentless and unforgiving. Dragonwülf and Morning Fire were undaunted, their bond giving them strength beyond measure.

"We shall not falter, Morning Fire! Together, we shall vanquish our foes and protect Jyr'dil!" Dragonwülf declared, his sword gleaming in the sunlight. "I will avenge you, brave warrior!"

The battle raged on, the sky filled with the clash of claws and the roar of the dragon. Morning Fire breathed streams of scorching flames, while Dragonwülf wielded his sword with expert skill, striking at the dragon's vulnerable spots. The air crackled with magic and power as the combatants fought with all their might.

As good vs. evil locked in a deadly dance of claws and fangs, Dragonwülf and Morning Fire fought with unmatched skill and determination.

"Stay focused, Morning Fire! We must find this demon's weak spot and strike swiftly," Dragonwülf shouted above the din of battle, his voice unwavering.

Morning Fire nodded in acknowledgment, his eyes never leaving their adversary. "I see it! Aim for **his** eyes, where the armor is weakest."

With a nod of understanding, Dragonwülf steered Morning Fire towards the vulnerable spot, dodging the dark demon's attacks with uncanny agility. As they closed in for the final strike, Ogor let out a deafening roar of defiance.

"I am an eternal being, born of fire and darkness!" roared Ogor.

"You can be defeated just as any other demon!" Dragonwülf and Morning Fire were undeterred, their bond of trust and companionship proving stronger than any supernatural power. With a mighty thrust, Dragonwülf plunged his sword deep into the beast's eye, striking true.

A blinding light engulfed the battlefield as the powerful Ogor let out a final, agonized scream. Its form began to disintegrate, vanishing into the ether as if it had never existed.

As soon as Ogor disappeared into the atmosphere, the Götterdämmerung fired all her rockets, shot up through the sky, and out into the distance.

"I should have known he would not stay to do battle with us!" said Dragonwülf to Morning Fire. "We are too much for him, are we not, my dragon friend? The Defiler is a coward."

Morning Fire roared in triumph, his eyes shining with pride."

As a guardian of the meek, Dragonwülf's legend lived on in Jyr'dil, a beacon of hope for those who cherished the tapestry of history and the sanctity of the ages. The name Lyra would be remembered through the annals of time, a testament to the courage and determination of a leader and a woman among men and women who had stood against The Defiler to protect her people.

In another part of the Universe in another time dimension, another evil demon raised his head in the annals of time. He was a Private in the Armed Forces of Germany. He was a frustrated painter of canvas who did not receive the recognition he felt he deserved. Soon, he would be the reason for another horrible war on the planet Earth. Dragonwülf knew that he must join the Deepwater Watchman at once and address this evil one.

The brisk wind whipped through Dragonwülf's long, braided beard as he made his way through the icy Nordic landscape of Arom near Asgard. His muscles tensed beneath his fur-lined armor as he quickened his pace, a sense of urgency burning within him.

As Dragonwülf crested a snow-covered hill, he caught sight of the flickering flames of a distant village. Smoke billowed into the gray sky, a stark contrast to the peaceful serenity of the surrounding forests. With a growl of determination, the Norse warrior picked up his pace, knowing he was running out of time.

Upon reaching the village, Dragonwülf was met with a scene of chaos and destruction. Buildings lay in ruins, their thatched roofs ablaze. Bodies littered the streets, the stench of death heavy in the air. The warrior's heart sank as he realized he was too late. The Defiler had been here, and his evil had left an indelible mark.

Amidst the devastation, Dragonwülf spotted a group of survivors huddled together near the town square. They looked to him with a mix of fear and hope, knowing that he was their only chance at salvation.

"Dragonwülf," a grizzled elderly man stepped forward, his voice trembling with emotion. "You must hurry. The Defiler has already made his move. He will unleash great evil upon the world."

The warrior's jaw clenched as he listened intently. "What has he done?" Dragonwülf demanded, his voice a low rumble that seemed to shake the very ground beneath their feet.

The elderly man's eyes darkened with sorrow. "He has traveled forward in time and altered the course of history. An evil man will reign as the leader of a land called Germany; his tyranny will spread like a plague across the lands."

Dragonwülf felt a surge of anger and despair wash over him. Adolph Hitler was a name whispered in fear and loathing throughout the ages, a symbol of unspeakable cruelty and hatred. The thought of such a man wielding power unchecked filled the warrior with a sense of grim foreboding.

"We must stop him," Dragonwülf vowed, his eyes burning with determination. "I will journey forward and confront The Defiler, no matter the cost."

With a heavy heart, the Norse warrior bid farewell to the survivors, his mind already racing with plans and strategies. He knew the road ahead would be fraught with danger and uncertainty, but he also knew that he could not stand idly by while evil triumphed.

As Dragonwülf set out on his quest to right the wrongs of the past, the very fabric of time seemed to ripple and bend around him. His fate was entwined with that of the world, his courage and valor serving as a beacon of hope in the face of overwhelming darkness. Though the path ahead was shrouded in shadows, the warrior pressed on, knowing that his actions would determine the course of history itself.

In the heart of the Universe of time in the folds of the panorama, the legendary Norse warrior Dragonwülf stood before his loyal crew of the mighty ship, the Deepwater Watchman. The air was thick with anticipation as the warriors gathered to make plans for their upcoming journey into the unknown territories of the Second World War.

With a fierce look in his eyes, Dragonwülf addressed his crew, his voice booming across the wooden docks. "Brothers of the Deepwater Watchman, the time has come for us to embark on a journey like no other. We shall sail into the depths of war, facing challenges that will test our strength and courage in ways we have never known."

As the crew gathered around a crackling fire on the deck of the long ship, Dragonwülf called upon the spirits of their ancestors for guidance. "Great Tyr, hear our plea. Grant us the strength to face our enemies and emerge victorious in the battles that lie ahead."

Suddenly, a powerful gust of wind swept across the ship, causing the flames to flicker and dance. The crew looked on in awe as a figure materialized from the shadows, clad in armor that shone like silver in the moonlight. It was the figure of Tyr, the god of war and weapons.

"I have heard your call, brave warriors and assassins," boomed Tyr, his voice resonating with power. "The path you have chosen is fraught with danger, but fear not, for I shall grant you my blessings in the battles to come."

The crew bowed their heads in reverence, their hearts filled with a newfound sense of courage and purpose. As Tyr faded back into the night, Dragonwülf turned to his crew, a fierce glint in his eye. "We have been chosen by the gods themselves to be warriors in this great conflict. Let us sail into battle with pride in our hearts and the spirit of our ancestors guiding us."

Therefore, with the blessings of Tyr and Róthul-Orkr, the crew of the Deepwater Watchman sailed forth into the heart of World War II, ready to face whatever challenges lay in their path.

Artifact Seven

Róthul-Orkr and the Bismarck

rþulorkr ok bismarkr

ᚱᚦᚢᛏᚩᚱᚲᚱ ᚩᚲ ᛒᛁᛋᛗᚨᚱᚲᚱ

Dimension of Loki May 26-27, 1941 CE Earth

"Die großen Fragen der Zeit werden nicht durch Reden und Majoritätsbeschlüsse entschieden, sondern durch Eisen und Blut."

"The great questions of the day will not be settled through speeches and majority decisions but by iron and blood."

-Otto von Bismarck. *(30, Sept 1862).*

The sun was setting over the vast horizon, painting the sky in hues of orange and pink as the HMS Hood and the legendary German battleship Bismarck faced off in the cold North Atlantic Ocean. The tension was palpable as the two mighty warships prepared for battle, their crews poised for the inevitable conflict that awaited them.

On the deck of the HMS Hood, Captain John stood tall, his gaze fixed on the approaching enemy. Beside him, Lieutenant Thomas scanned the horizon through his binoculars, his heart pounding with anticipation.

"They're closing in, Sir," Thomas whispered, his voice tinged with nervous excitement.

Captain John nodded, his jaw set in determination. "Prepare the guns. We'll give them everything we've got."

As the ships drew closer, the Bismarck unleashed a barrage of firepower, sending explosions and plumes of smoke into the air. The HMS Hood responded in kind, the deafening roar of its guns filling the air.

"Fire!" Captain John bellowed, his voice cutting through the chaos of battle.

The cannons of the HMS Hood rumbled to life, sending projectiles hurtling towards the Bismarck. The German ship was a formidable opponent, its armor holding strong against the onslaught.

Suddenly, a sharp crack split the air as a projectile from the Bismarck found its mark on the HMS Hood, piercing through its hull with deadly precision. The explosion that followed was like a thunderclap, shaking the very ocean itself as flames engulfed the doomed ship.

"No...," Captain John whispered, his voice barely audible over the sounds of destruction.

The HMS Hood was engulfed in flames, its once-proud structure torn asunder by the devastating blow. As the crew scrambled to abandon ship, the Bismarck loomed in the distance, a silent witness to the destruction it had wrought.

In the aftermath of the battle, as the smoke cleared and the remains of the HMS Hood slipped beneath the waves, Captain John stood on the deck of a rescue ship, his eyes fixed on the horizon where the Bismarck had disappeared.

Róthul-Orkr, the Whale God

Dragonwülf was a force to be reckoned with, carrying the burden of a mission - to protect the Earth from the wrath of a malicious being. However, the ancient warrior was constantly tormented by immense doubt. He questioned if his mission was unfeigned or simply a fruitless endeavor imposed upon him by a commanding power. As despair threatened to consume him, he walked the calming deck of the Deepwater Watchman, grappling with his eternal quest.

One night, under the iridescent glow of moonlight, there appeared a colossal entity from the cerulean depths. The sea shimmered under its gigantic shadow, stirring waves of awe and fear within Dragonwülf. Majestically, the entity revealed itself as Róthul-Orkr, the revered Whale God of ancient lore. Its imposing azure eyes shimmered with wisdom, striking a chord of reverence in Dragonwülf's heart.

"Fear not, Dragonwülf," boomed the resonant voice of Róthul-Orkr echoing against the waves, "for I have come to help you navigate the troubled waters of uncertainty."

Dragonwülf bowed before the divine apparition. "Grateful I am, O mighty one, for your heed. What reason does a power this supreme have to converse with a mere mortal? Where have you been all of my life when I needed your help? Forgive me, O mighty one, but I felt forsaken. I even believed you did not exist. I am really embarrassed."

"Even the mightiest beings," Róthul-Orkr began, "understand the value of unity and counsel. I was always with you, even in the loneliest of times. The ocean does not scorn the simple ones like yourself, but instead, we revel in raising you to greatness. Carry the weight of your actions with pride, not regret," began the Whale God. "Even the tiniest droplets contribute to the boundless ocean. Every decision you make carries the power to turn tides just as every battle you fight contributes to the larger war against malevolence."

"Secondly," Róthul-Orkr continued, "navigate through life with the virtue of patience. Even the greatest storms are surrendered to the serenity of time, and the biggest whales do not rush through the water; they glide with grace and power. Patience, my brave warrior, will triumph over haste."

"Finally," the Whale God concluded, "Remember that you are the ocean and not the tempest. Though tragedies may shake you and adversaries may try to swallow you, they are but transient. You, Dragonwülf, the embodiment of valor and resilience, are meant for permanence."

"What would you have me do, O' great one?" asked Dragonwülf." I am at your service."

"Upon the sea, there is a monster disguised as a battleship. Your Deepwater Watchman could rest in a part of the aft of this ship. She is called The Bismarck, and she is a creation of The Defiler."

"What am I to do against this behemoth of a ship? There are only cannons aboard the Watchman," noted Dragonwülf.

"I will give you the HMS Hood. Bismarck sent her to the murky bottom of the sea. I would like you to return to your ship and enter the Panorama at the time of battle aboard the Hood. Trust the crew, and I will be at your Service," promised the Róthul-Orkr.

⸻⬥⬦⬥⸻

Aboard the Deepwater Watchman, Dragonwülf appeared amongst his crew and Captain Old-Turas.

"There is a great war on the earth, Captain," said Dragonwülf. A great and formidable weapon is being wielded by The Defiler, and we must destroy it. I require assistance from The Destiny of Tyr. Most of all, I require the help of the greatest sea Captain of the seven seas. Do you know anyone who could do that?"

"Aye. When do we leave?" answered the salty sea dog.

"We have the support of Róthul-Orkr and a promise he will be there," said Dragonwülf.

"There you go again with your hope in false gods. You spoke of your disappointment in your gods many times."

"This is different. Come and see," said the old warrior. "We must send this evil ship to the bottom of the ocean. We will then end the war by removing the head of the Defiler. I swear by all that is sacred, I will have his miserable head."

"The time approaches!" said Avat'or. "You must leap into the Panorama soon."

"Stay close, Turas!" shouted Dragonwülf as he and the Captain were hurled from the Panorama onto the deck of the HMS Hood.

The warrior and the Captain found themselves in the vast Atlantic Ocean during WWII. Dragonwülf and Captain Old Turas found themselves in the midst of the Battle of the Denmark Strait on May 24, 1941. Historically, the German battleship Bismarck sank the British battlecruiser HMS Hood that day. The Bismarck scored a single hit that caused the Hood's magazines to explode, sinking the ship in just a few minutes. Today, Dragonwülf and his god Róthul-Orkr would see a different outcome.

The prestigious HMS Hood sailed proudly, its crew ready for any battle that came their way. Across the waters, the formidable German battleship Bismarck loomed, a force to be reckoned with. The tension between the two ships was palpable, as the fate of the seas seemed to be uncertain.

As the Hood and the Bismarck faced off, the atmosphere was charged with anticipation. The captains of both ships, Admiral Holland of the Hood and Admiral Lütjens of the Bismarck, stood on their respective decks, their steely gazes locked in a battle of wills. Captain Müller was at the helm of the deadly German ship.

"Prepare for battle, men!" shouted Admiral Holland, his voice echoing across the deck. "We shall show Bismarck what the HMS Hood is made of!"

The crew of the Hood sprang into action, their training and discipline evident as they readied their weapons and prepared for the impending clash. On the Bismarck, the sailors worked swiftly and efficiently, their determination matching that of their rivals.

Just as the two mighty ships closed in on each other, two figures unlike any other appeared on the deck of the HMS Hood.

"I am Dragonwülf, son of Óðinn, here to aid you in this battle," he declared, his eyes ablaze with fervor.

"Aye!"-said Turas. "The Captain of the North Hundren, which lies at the bottom of the sea, at your Service."

Admiral Holland, though taken aback, welcomed the help, knowing that they would need all the assistance they could get against the Bismarck.

The battle raged on, the thunder of cannons and the clash of steel filling the air. The Bismarck unleashed its firepower upon the HMS Hood, causing damage to its hull. The crew of the Hood fought back with unwavering resolve, their courage unwavering.

Amidst the chaos, Dragonwülf called upon his god, Róthul-Orkr. With a thunderous roar, Róthul-Orkr emerged from the depths, his immense form towering over the ocean. The sea itself seemed to heed his command, rising and crashing upon the Bismarck with ferocity.

The waves crashed against the massive hull of the German Battle cruiser, the Bismarck, as it sailed through the treacherous waters of the North Atlantic. On board, Captain Müller stood on the deck, his gaze fixed on the horizon. Suddenly, a shadow loomed over the ship, casting a dark cloud over the entire crew.

"What in the world is that?" one of the sailors exclaimed, pointing toward the sea.

As the crew turned their attention to the water, they gasped in horror at the sight before them. Rising from the depths was a colossal figure, larger than any whale they had ever seen. Its body was covered in shimmering and shining skin that glowed with an otherworldly light, and its eyes burned with a fierce intensity.

"It's a damned huge killer whale," Captain Müller whispered, his voice filled with fear and awe.

The massive creature let out a deafening roar that shook the very foundations of the ship. The crew scrambled into action, desperately trying to steer the vessel away from the wrath of the ancient being. Nevertheless, it was futile. The Whale God seemed to control the very waters themselves, guiding the ship toward its inevitable doom.

"Abandon ship!" Captain Müller yelled his voice barely audible over the howling winds and crashing waves.

As the crew leaped into the icy waters, the Whale God reared up, towering over the ship like a vengeful deity. With a swift motion of its tail, it struck the hull of The Bismarck, tearing through the metal with ease. The once mighty vessel groaned and shuddered, its fate sealed by the wrath of the ancient being.

In a spectacular display of power and fury, the Whale God unleashed a torrent of energy that enveloped Bismarck in a blinding light. The ship buckled and twisted under the immense force before finally succumbing to the depths below.

As the last remnants of The Bismarck disappeared beneath the waves, The Whale God let out a haunting cry that echoed across the ocean. The crew watched in stunned silence as the creature slowly descended back into the depths, leaving only ripples in its wake.

The Whale God vanished once more, a fearsome reminder of the power that dwells beneath the surface of the North Atlantic. The crew clung to rafts and debris, their hearts heavy with the memory of the epic battle that had unfolded before their very eyes. Even as they were rescued by passing ships, they knew that they would never forget the day they witnessed the awesome might of The Whale God.

"Feel the wrath of the sea, Bismarck!" Dragonwülf cried, his voice carrying over the tumultuous waters.

The combined might of the HMS Hood, Dragonwülf, and Róthul-Orkr proved to be too much for the Bismarck to withstand. With a final, resounding blast, the Bismarck was dealt a fatal blow, its fate sealed in the depths below.

Artifact Eight

To Berlin

Date Dimension of Loki 1942 CE
World War II

I will never go to someone's golden shores or planet again just to kill them, but… in your case, I will make an exception."
Jarvis Nightwish

In a cacophony of swirling lights and crackling energy, Dragonwülf, Captain Old Turas, Jarvis Nightwish, and Viktor Vorobyev found themselves standing in the heart of a war-torn Berlin, circa World War II. The air was thick with the acrid scent of smoke, and the distant rumble of explosions echoed through the cobblestone streets.

"The Defiler has a puppet in the person of Adolph Hitler, and he must be stopped," said Dragonwülf to his willing crew.

As they made their way through the desolate city, they encountered a group of Nazi soldiers blocking their path. The soldiers hesitated, unsure of how to respond to the strange group before them. Jarvis Nightwish, the cunning executioner of the group, stepped in. With a flourish of his hands, he conjured his disruptor, distracting the soldiers.

He stood tall, his eyes gleaming with a fierce determination. Clad in his dark trench coat and a hat pulled low over his eyes, he held in his hands a weapon unlike any other - the Disruptor. This weapon had the power to reduce any living being to ashes with a single touch.

The German soldiers seemed unaffected. Their guns aimed at him, Jarvis calmly raised the Disruptor. The soldiers hesitated, sensing the deadly power emanating from the weapon.

"You have made a grave mistake by crossing paths with me," Jarvis said, his voice low and menacing. "But fear not, for your end will be swift."

The soldiers exchanged worried glances but managed a laugh or two.

"What is this toy gun that this man has threatened us with?" said soldier Peter. "What is the strange clothing you wear? Why are you dressed like this in Berlin?"

"Shoot them now," ordered the higher-ranking officer.

. They continued to advance, their movements cautious.

With a steady hand, Jarvis slowly extended the Disruptor towards the soldiers, the weapon humming with energy. Sparks flew from the barrel, crackling with an ominous intensity.

"Any last words?" Jarvis asked with a wicked grin, his finger hovering over the trigger.

One of the soldiers, a young man with fear in his eyes, spoke up. "What is this weapon?" he said with trepidation.

Jarvis narrowed his eyes, considering the question for a moment. He knew all too well the horrors these soldiers had committed in the name of their cause. He could not show mercy to those who had shown none themselves.

Without a word, Jarvis pressed the trigger of the Disruptor. A blinding flash of light erupted from the weapon, engulfing the soldiers in a searing blaze. Their screams echoed through the battlefield as their bodies disintegrated into ash, carried away by the wind.

As the smoke cleared, Jarvis stood alone amongst the remnants of his enemies, the Disruptor still crackling with power in his hand. He gazed upon the destruction he had wrought, a mix of satisfaction and sorrow in his eyes.

"The Disruptor never fails," Jarvis muttered to himself.

"That is a weapon I could have used to defeat many enemies over the years. I am jealous of the power you wield," said Dragonwülf. "When we return to the Watchman, I want to barter with you for it."

"I will never part with the Disruptor. It is an extension of my arm. We will defeat the Defiler using its power."

———◆◆◆———

According to the records kept by The Destiny of Tyr, this would not be the first assassination plot on the life of the Feurer. Forty-two of these plots had already ended in failure.

"You must not fail. There is still time to save countless lives, Ser Dragonwülf," stated Avat'or.

One particular event seemed to mirror all of the rest of the attempts, placing Hitler usually in the right place at the wrong time, inevitably saving his life.

On November 8, 1939, would-be bomber Georg Elser paced nervously in his small workshop, the dim light casting long shadows on the walls. The ticking of the clock on the wall seemed to echo the pounding of his heart as he made final adjustments to the homemade explosive device in front of him. He had been planning this for months, meticulously calculating every detail, ensuring that his bomb would go off at precisely the right moment.

His mind raced with thoughts of the injustice and tyranny that had consumed his beloved country. Hitler's rise to power had brought nothing but suffering and oppression to the German people, and Elser was determined to put an end to it all.

As the clock struck 7:30, Elser took a deep breath and grabbed the bomb. He carefully concealed it in his coat and made his way to the Bürgerbräukeller Beer Hall, where Hitler was scheduled to give a speech that evening.

Inside the crowded hall, the atmosphere was tense with anticipation. Elser blended into the sea of eager faces, his heart pounding in his chest. He watched as Hitler took the stage, his voice booming with hatred and arrogance. The audience erupted into cheers, but Elser felt nothing but disgust.

As Hitler's speech droned on, Elser's grip on the bomb tightened. Every second felt like an eternity as he waited for the perfect moment to strike. Suddenly, Hitler announced that he would be cutting his speech short and would be leaving in just a few minutes.

Panic surged through Elser as he realized that his carefully calculated plan was about to fall apart. He had planned for Hitler to stay until at least 21:00, giving him enough time to escape before the bomb went off.

Frantically, Elser scanned the room, searching for the right opportunity. Finally, at 20:55, he saw his chance. Hitler finished his speech and began to make his way towards the exit, flanked by his entourage.

With a surge of determination, Elser reached into his coat and pulled out the bomb. He threw it towards the stage, his heart pounding in his ears. The bomb flew through the air, a fiery blur of metal and destruction.

Time seemed to slow as the bomb hurtled towards its target. The room erupted into chaos as people screamed and scrambled for cover. With a deafening roar, the bomb exploded, sending shockwaves through the hall.

The pillar detonated in a shower of debris, and a section of the roof collapsed onto the stage where Hitler had been standing just moments before. Smoke filled the air, obscuring the chaos and confusion that followed.

As the dust began to settle, Elser emerged from the mayhem, his face streaked with soot and sweat. He looked around at the destruction he had caused, his heart heavy but his spirit unbroken.

At that moment, Georg Elser knew that his act of defiance had not brought about the end of Hitler's reign of terror. He also knew that he had done everything in his power to stand up against tyranny and fight for the freedom of his people.

As he was dragged away by the authorities, a faint smile played on his lips, a smile that spoke of courage, resilience, and unwavering determination in the face of insurmountable odds. Elser was held as a prisoner for over five years until he was executed at the Dachau concentration camp less than a month before the surrender of Nazi Germany.

"Let the story of this brave man be a lesson for you, Ser Dragonwülf. These plots have a high failure rate," said Avat'or.

"We will avenge you, Ser Elser, son of your father and brother of all." I swear it," said Dragonwülf.

"You must know of one other plot to take the life of this monster that is a puppet of The Defiler," warned Avat'or.

Claus von Stauffenberg paced nervously in the courtyard of a grand building in Berlin, his co-conspirators gathered around him, their faces etched with a mixture of determination and fear.

"This is it, gentlemen," Stauffenberg declared, his voice unwavering despite the swirling emotions inside him. "Today, we make our stand against tyranny."

The others nodded solemnly, their eyes reflecting the gravity of the situation. They knew that failure would mean certain death, but they were willing to risk it all for the greater good.

Hours later, Stauffenberg put the plan into action on July 20, 1944. He and his fellow officials were called to a conference with Hitler at the Wolf's Lair, the dictator's heavily guarded headquarters in East Prussia.

Inside the conference room, tension hung heavy in the air as Hitler ranted about his plans for the war. Stauffenberg felt a surge of adrenaline as he reached for the briefcase strapped to his side, the weight of his mission pressing down on him.

As he positioned himself near Hitler, his heart pounded in his chest. With steady hands, he set the briefcase down, the plastic explosives hidden within primed and ready to detonate.

A heated discussion erupted in the room, providing the perfect cover for Stauffenberg to slip away unnoticed. He excused himself under the guise of needing to make an important phone call, his every step calculated and precise.

Outside, he waited, his eyes fixed on the building that held the fate of the world in its grip. Minutes passed like hours until, suddenly, a deafening explosion shattered the silence.

The force of the blast was immense, shattering windows and sending shockwaves through the earth. The conference room was engulfed in chaos, the smell of smoke and burning debris filling the air.

Stauffenberg felt a surge of relief cover him. At first, he believed that he had accomplished his mission. Four men lay dead, but Hitler had miraculously survived, though wounded by the blast.

As the dust settled, chaos reigned within the Wolf's Lair. Stauffenberg's heart raced as he tried to make his way to safety, his mind swirling with a mix of emotions. Victory and defeat intertwined in a complex dance, leaving him breathless and uncertain of what the future held.

Despite his best efforts to evade capture, Stauffenberg and the rest of the conspirators were eventually rounded up by the SS. They were interrogated, tortured, and ultimately executed for their roles in the failed assassination attempt.

"The name of Stauffenberg will live in infamy as one of the bravest soldiers in history for his supreme sacrifice," said Avat'or.

"I promise you we will not fail," said Luciano. "Today we're gonna whack Hitler! If the boys in my crew could see this, they would not believe it!"

"He will not escape my disruptor," said Nightwish.

"Or my pistol," said Viktor. My parents were Ukrainian immigrants, and this is personal."

———⬥⬥⬥———

In a dimly lit alleyway in the heart of Berlin, Dragonwülf, Viktor Vorobyev, Jarvis Nightwish, and Captain Turas stood nervously outside a nondescript building. They were about to infiltrate the office of Adolph Hitler, the most feared man in all of Europe. Dressed in their finest suits and carrying forged documents, they were posing as art dealers on a mission to bring down the tyrant. The Destiny of Tyr understood Hitler's obsession with fine art.

As they entered Hitler's office, they were met with a chilling silence. The room was adorned with paintings and sculptures, a stark contrast to the evil that resided within its walls. At the far end of the room, sitting behind a grand desk, was the man himself - a cruel smirk playing on his lips.

"Ah, my dear art dealers," Hitler sneered. "What brings you to me today?"

Dragonwülf, the leader of the group, stepped forward confidently. "We have come to present to you a piece of art that will change the course of history," he declared.

Hitler's eyes gleamed with curiosity. "Oh? And what might this piece be?"

Vorobyev unveiled a painting from his case. It depicted a scene of chaos and destruction, with a ferocious dragon breathing fire onto a field of swastikas.

"This, *Führer*, is the Dragon of Justice," Vorobyev explained. "It symbolizes the end of tyranny and the rise of freedom."

Hitler's facade of calmness cracked, his eyes widening in shock and rage. "How dare you bring such blasphemy into my presence!" he roared.

Jarvis Nightwish, the cunning strategist, stepped in.

"But Herr Hitler, this painting is not just art. It is a prophecy of your downfall." Nightwish wielded the disruptor in his hand, a weapon of immense power capable of disintegrating anything it touched.

"You stand accused of crimes against humanity," Jarvis declared, his voice echoing ominously in the chamber. "It is time for you to face justice."

Hitler glared back at Jarvis with hatred in his eyes. "You will never succeed. My legacy will live on, and you will never extinguish the fire I have ignited."

Jarvis raised the disruptor and aimed it at Hitler. With a steady hand, he pulled the trigger, and a beam of energy shot forth, enveloping Hitler's body. The tyrant's screams filled the chamber as his form began to disintegrate, not leaving behind ashes, but simply fading away into nothingness.

The echo of Hitler's shrieks seemed to stretch into eternity, a haunting reminder of the evil that had once resided within the chamber. Jarvis closed his eyes, his heart heavy with the weight of what he had just done.

As the last remnants of Hitler's existence faded away, a profound silence descended upon the chamber. Jarvis lowered the disruptor, his task now complete.

Jarvis Nightwish, the executioner of the temple on Saturn's moon, turned and walked away, leaving behind only the echoes of Adolf Hitler's final moments, lost to eternity.

Artifact Nine

Ásjá and the Planet Destroyer

Date: Future Dimension of Thor 2396 CE

"I would rather die fighting than live in submission to a tyrant!"

The Defiler, a being cloaked in darkness and draped in shadows, sat on the throne of the Götterdämmerung, the planet destroyer that loomed like a sinister specter in the vastness of space. His form was a twisted amalgamation of alien and demonic features, his eyes glowed with an otherworldly light, his skin a sickly shade of onyx that seemed to absorb the very essence of light around him.

Surrounded by his legion of devoted minions, each one more grotesque and terrifying than the last, The Defiler raised a clawed hand and commanded in a voice that echoed with the whispers of a thousand damned souls, "Prepare the *Dark Star* cannon for firing. We shall bring chaos and destruction to the cosmos, and none shall stand in our way. The planet that lies before us is the planet Phobos, with nearly one billion inhabitants. We will destroy all in our path," he said while laughing a sinister laugh of death.

As the crew scurried to carry out his orders, a brave crew person named Ásjá (Protection) stepped away from her post, determined to stop The Defiler and his malevolent plans. She was a warrior with a heart as fierce as a burning star, her golden armor gleaming in stark contrast to the shadows that enveloped the ship.

Ásjá confronted The Defiler, her sword drawn and determination etched into her every movement. "You will not succeed, you creature of darkness," she declared, her voice unwavering despite the looming threat before her. "You cannot destroy a planet! When we joined you, it was in search of treasure and plunder. We are not genocidal maniacs!" Ásjác said in a pleading tone.

"You dare mutiny on my ship! Now you will die! Are there any among you who wish to join her?

The Defiler turned to face her, a twisted smile curling his lips as he regarded this lone warrior standing against him. "Ah, the valiant Ásjá," he hissed, his eyes glittering with curiosity. "You are but a nuisance in my grand design. Prepare to be obliterated along with all who dare to defy me. You have forgotten that I taught you all that you know. You owe your life to me, and now I will collect it!"

A fierce battle erupted between Ásjá and The Defiler, the clash of swords and the crackle of dark magic filling the air as their two opposing forces clashed. The minions of henchmen watched in awe and fear, unsure of who would emerge victorious in this ultimate confrontation.

Ásjá, with her shimmering silver armor and determined eyes, raised her sword high, ready to strike. "You will not destroy this planet, not on my watch!" she shouted, her voice resolute.

The Defiler, a sinister figure cloaked in shadow, sneered. "You cannot stop me, Ásjá. My power is unmatched, and this planet will fall at my feet. Are you not aware that I am a god?" he bellowed.

The two charged at each other, their swords meeting with a deafening clang. The force of their impact sent shockwaves through the ship, causing alarms to blare and lights to flicker ominously.

Ásjá gritted her teeth, pushing back against The Defiler's overwhelming strength. "I will not let you bring ruin to this world! Your tyranny ends here!"

The Defiler laughed darkly, his eyes glowing with malevolence. "You are a fool to challenge me. You cannot comprehend the depth of power I wield."

As the battle raged on, the crew of the Götterdämmerung watched in awe and fear. They knew that the outcome of this duel would determine the fate of not just their ship, but also the entire planet below.

Ásjá fought with all her might, her sword dancing with precision and skill.

The Defiler's attacks grew more vicious, his malevolent laughter echoing through the chamber. "There is no hope for you. Surrender now, and perhaps I will spare your life."

The battle reached its peak, the clash of their swords ringing out like thunder. Sparks flew as Ásjá and The Defiler locked in a fierce struggle, each refusing to back down. Their blades danced in the air, a symphony of clashing metal and sparks.

Ásjá gritted her teeth, determination blazing in her eyes. "You will never win, Defiler! I will fight for that planet!"

The Defiler chuckled darkly, his voice dripping with malice as he parried her strikes effortlessly. "Foolish girl, your resistance is futile. The power of the Götterdämmerung is unmatched. Surrender now, and I may spare your life."

Ásjá's gaze hardened, her grip on her sword tightening. "I would rather die fighting than live in submission to tyrants like you!"

The battle raged on, each combatant pushing themselves to their limits. The Defiler's ominous laughter filled the air as he gained the upper hand, slowly driving Ásjá back towards the edge of the platform.

"You are strong, warrior, but strength alone cannot save you," the Defiler taunted, his eyes gleaming with malevolence.

Ásjá's back hit the railing, the vast expanse of space stretching out beyond it. She glanced behind her for a fleeting moment before focusing back on her opponent, a fierce determination burning in her soul.

The Defiler's smirk faltered for a brief moment as he recognized the unwavering resolve in Ásjá's eyes. He lunged forward, aiming to deliver the final blow, but Ásjá swiftly sidestepped his attack, her movements fluid and precise.

With a swift motion, she swung her sword with all her strength, a blinding flash of light illuminating the chamber as the blade connected with the Defiler's armor. The Defiler lunged forward and caught the center of her chest with a jagged claw, causing her to topple into the void of space. The crew of the planet destroyer could hear her shrieks as she disappeared into black space.

"Are there any more among you who wish to mutiny today?" asked the Defiler. His question was met with silence. "Very well, then, ready the Dark Star at once! The people of Phobos await their doom!"

"We are ready to initiate the firing sequence, my Lord," a robotic voice intoned.

The Defiler nodded, his expression cold and unyielding. "Do it. Show them the price of defying us."

As the Dark Star hummed to life, a brilliant beam of dark energy shot out from the colossal ship, streaking across the void of space toward the doomed planet. On Phobos, panic and chaos ensued as the inhabitants realized their impending destruction.

"No! Please, you must not do this!" cried out a desperate voice over the planetary channels.

"I offered to let your planet live in exchange for worship as your god. You rejected me. Now you will pay for your insolence!"

The Defiler watched with a twisted grin as Phobos was consumed by a cataclysmic explosion, reduced to rubble and ash in a matter of seconds. The destruction was absolute, a testament to the power he wielded.

"Excellent," he murmured, a note of satisfaction in his voice. "Let this be a lesson to all who dare to oppose us. None shall stand in our way."

As the crew aboard the Götterdämmerung prepared to continue on their voyage of doom, a lone figure approached the Defiler. It was his second-in-command, a ruthless warrior known as Bell'ore.

"My Lord, I must admit, even I am in awe of the destructive force of the Dark Star," Bell'ore said, his voice filled with a mixture of admiration and fear.

The Defiler turned to him, his gaze piercing. "Fear not. With this weapon at our disposal, we will crush all who oppose us and bring the galaxy to its knees."

"But at what cost, my Lord? How many lives will be lost in our pursuit of power?" Bell'ore asked, his tone challenging.

The Defiler's eyes narrowed, a flicker of emotion crossing his face. "The cost is irrelevant. We are destined for greatness, and sacrifices must be made. It is the price of our ascension."

With a final look at the now lifeless husk that was once Phobos, the Defiler turned away, his heart as cold and unyielding as the void of space itself. The Dark Star had spoken, and its message was one of destruction and despair. As long as he held his power in his grasp, none would be safe from his wrath. Some of the crew would remember the sacrifice that was made on this day aboard the Götterdämmerung, the planet destroyer. Ásjá's name would be forever remembered as the warrior who tried to save her world from destruction.

Artifact Nine

Luciano's Vendetta

Date: Dimension of Loki 1987 AD
Earth, New York City

"In the echoes of the past, I hear her voice.
Forgive me for what I have become, Mama."
- Luciano Cantore.

On the deck of the Deepwater Watchman, as the rest of the men drank from tankards, Dragonwülf considered one of his companions with great curiosity.

Luciano Cantore sat on the dimly lit deck, his gaze fixed on Dragonwülf. His seasoned eyes scanned the ship, noticing the various men lost in their own conversations and mugs of ale. The clinking of tankards and the murmur of voices formed a comforting background noise for the weary assassin.

As he sipped on his drink, Dragonwülf's piercing gaze met Luciano's, and a tense silence settled between a skilled warrior and a killer. Luciano inclined his head slightly, acknowledging the other's presence.

"You are the Shadow blade of the East," Dragonwülf spoke in a low, gravelly voice that carried an air of authority. "That is what I will call you."

Luciano nodded, a flicker of curiosity sparking in his eyes.

"Why are you so interested in me?"

Dragonwülf's lips curled into a faint smirk. "Let us just say I have an interest in those who walk the shadowed path of an assassin. Tell me, Luciano, what drives you to take a life? Is it for coin, for vengeance, or for something else entirely?"

Luciano leaned back in his chair, contemplating the question. "I believe that an assassin is both a sword and a mirror. We are weapons honed by our pasts, reflecting the darkness that lies within us. We also have the power to shape our own destinies, to decide whether we are bound by our sins or redeemed by our actions."

Dragonwülf's expression remained unreadable as he listened to Luciano's words. "A poetic sentiment, but do you not find it a lonely existence, to walk the shadows and bear the weight of death on your shoulders?"

Luciano's eyes hardened, a shadow passing over his features. "Loneliness is a small price to pay for the freedom that comes with embracing the shadows. We are the whispers in the dark, the unseen hands that shape the course of history. Our solitude is a small sacrifice for the power we wield."

As the night wore on, Luciano and Dragonwülf shared tales of their past deeds and whispered of the mysteries that shrouded their world.

"It is time for the Shadow blade of the East to reconcile his timeline," said Dragonwülf. We are nearing the portal for your redemption. Prepare yourself for what is to come!"

In a flash of light, Luciano Cantore, known throughout the underworld for his ruthless efficiency and unwavering loyalty, found himself instantly lying in a pool of his own blood, betrayed by the one person he trusted the most - his brother, Sal. As he slowly regained consciousness, Luciano's thoughts were consumed by a searing thirst for vengeance. He was no longer on the Deepwater Watchman but rather in another realm.

With a steely determination in his eyes, Luciano began to plot his revenge against Sal. He bided his time, allowing his wounds to heal and his strength to return, all the while keeping a low profile to avoid drawing unwanted attention from the authorities.

"Sal may have thought he got rid of me, but he just awakened the beast within. Revenge is a dish best served cold, and I intend to make him taste every bitter bite of it," he was overheard boasting.

Months passed, and Luciano's plan slowly took shape. He meticulously gathered information, leveraging his network of informants and allies to unearth Sal's whereabouts and daily routines. He knew that patience was important and that rushing into things would only jeopardize his chances of success.

Luciano's eyes scanned the bustling streets of 1980s New York City. The neon lights reflected off his polished dress shoes as he navigated the crowded sidewalks. The whispers of his past reverberated in his mind, a constant reminder of the life he had led before his untimely demise.

"You look lost, mister," a raspy voice cut through the cacophony of the city.

Luciano turned to see a weathered old man sitting on a stoop, a cigarette dangling from his lips. "I'm looking for answers," Luciano replied, his voice low and gruff.

The old man chuckled, smoke billowing from his nostrils. "Ain't we all, son? What kind of answers you lookin' for?"

With a sigh, Luciano sat beside the old man, the weight of his sins heavy on his shoulders. "I have a chance to right a wrong, to prevent my own death. But I don't know where to start."

The old man studied Luciano for a moment before speaking. "Death has a funny way of bringing clarity, doesn't it? Maybe you should start where it all began."

Memories flooded Luciano's mind - the dark alleys, the blood on his hands, the deals struck in shadows. He clenched his fists, a fire igniting within him. "I know where I must go."

Luciano Cantore stood in front of the bus stop glass booth, his reflection staring back at him with a mixture of determination and disbelief. "So, what you're saying is I have a chance to change my fate?" he muttered to the enigmatic figure standing beside him.

The figure, clad in a cloak that seemed to absorb all light, nodded solemnly. "Yes, Luciano. You have been chosen for this task because of your unique ability to navigate the shadows of the world. You must go back to 1982, to the night when your life was taken, and prevent it from happening."

"Who are you, old man?" asked a shocked Luciano.

"I have always been with you from the beginning of your life. I have prepared you for this time," the figure said.

"But who are you? What is your name?" asked Luciano.

"I have been known to you by many names. I was your Grandfather, Leo, I was Father Kelly, your priest, and many others," admitted the old man. "You were never alone. The Destiny of Tyr sent us to keep you safe. The world depends on you, Luciano. You and your comrades will deliver us safely through what is to come.

Luciano scoffed, his hand absentmindedly running over the scar that marred his cheek - a grim reminder of the violent end he had met. "And how exactly am I supposed to do that?

The figure's eyes glinted with an otherworldly light as he spoke, his voice echoing throughout the room. "You must find the one responsible for your demise and confront them. Only by facing your enemy head-on can you reclaim your life and set things right. Your balance will help the universe to be balanced and reconciled."

Without another word, the figure raised a hand, and a swirling vortex of light enveloped Luciano, pulling him back through time and space to the gritty streets of 1986 New York City.

As Luciano emerged from the vortex, he found himself surrounded by the neon glow of the city that never slept. The air was thick with the sounds of jazz music and distant sirens, a stark contrast to the silence that had enveloped him moments before.

Determined to fulfill his mission, Luciano set out into the night, his eyes scanning the faces of the countless individuals who passed him by. It was not long before he caught sight of a familiar figure - a young man with a cruel smile and eyes that held a glint of malice.

"Johnny," Luciano whispered, his voice filled with a mix of dread and recognition. It was his former associate, the man who had betrayed him and sealed his fate.

Johnny turned, his gaze locking onto Luciano's with a mixture of surprise and fear. "Luciano...I thought you were dead."

Luciano's jaw clenched as he approached his former partner, his every step filled with purpose. "Not yet, Johnny-boy…but if you don't tell me the truth about that night, I can guarantee you won't live to see another sunrise."

As the two men stood face to face, the echoes of their past sins reverberated through the night, blending with the jazz music that filled the air. In that moment, Luciano knew that his journey had only just begun - a journey to reclaim his life and rewrite the dark chapters of his fate.

Memories flooded Luciano's mind - the dark alleys, the blood on his hands, the deals struck in shadows. He clenched his fists, a fire igniting within him. Luciano glanced over his shoulder, his eyes reflecting the flickering neon lights of the city as he stood in an empty alleyway, the cold wind whispering through the narrow passageway. Johnny, his former partner, stood before him, a look of defiance in his eyes.

"You think you can just walk away from this?" Luciano's voice was low and dangerous, his hand hovering over the gun tucked into the waistband of his trousers.

Johnny smirked, a cruel twist of his lips. "I did what I had to do, Luciano. It's nothing personal."

Luciano's grip tightened on the gun. "Nothing personal, huh? You think you can betray me and get away with it?"

Johnny spread his hands, a mocking gesture. "You know how it is, Luciano. It's business, pure and simple."

Luciano's nostrils flared with anger. "Business? You call this business?" Without another word, he raised the gun and fired, the sound echoing through the alleyway.

Johnny staggered back, a look of shock on his face as blood blossomed on his chest. "You... you son of a..."

Luciano's expression was cold as he watched Johnny slump to the ground, his life ebbing away. "That's for betraying me, Johnny. That's for crossing the line."

As Johnny's eyes flickered closed, Luciano turned away, his footsteps echoing on the pavement as he disappeared into the night, leaving behind the echoes of his revenge.

As he made his way to the heart of the city, Luciano felt the eyes of the past watching him, judging him. He entered the dimly lit club, the thumping bass reverberating in his chest. The air was thick with smoke and tension, but Luciano strode through with purpose.

⚜

Finally, the day of reckoning arrived. Under the cover of darkness, Luciano stealthily made his way to Sal's hideout, his heart pounding with a mix of anticipation and rage. As he crept closer, he could hear the faint sounds of laughter and revelry emanating from within, a stark contrast to the turmoil brewing within his own soul.

With a silent grace befitting his years of training, Luciano slipped inside, moving like a shadow in the night. Then, at last, he came face to face with Sal, the man who had betrayed him in the most heinous of ways.

Their eyes locked in a silent exchange that spoke volumes. Luciano's gaze was icy, filled with a resolve that sent shivers down Sal's spine. At that moment, Sal knew that he was about to pay dearly for his treachery.

Without a word, Luciano swiftly drew his weapon, the cold steel glinting in the dim light. Sal's eyes widened in disbelief as he realized there were no escape plans and no way to undo the past.

"Luci, you're alive? That can't be you," a voice called out from the shadows.

Luciano's breath caught in his throat as he laid eyes on his younger brother, Sal, a look of shock and recognition crossing his face. "I've come to pay you back," Luciano said, his voice steady.

Luciano's eyes burned with the fire of vengeance as he confronted Sal, who looked at him with a mix of fear and regret.

"You thought you could kill me, but I've returned from the future to right your wrongs," Luciano declared, his voice low and dangerous.

Sal gulped nervously, knowing the danger his brother posed. "Bullcrap, there is no way that you could even be here, Luciano. I did kill you! You were as dead as a rock! There is no way this is real!"

"Oh yeah, it's real."

I never meant for things to go this far. Please, give me a chance to get away! I never meant," Sal pleaded, desperation evident in his voice.

"You never meant what?" asked Luciano. "You're a lyin' bag of trash!" Luciano balled his fist and punched Sal squarely in the jaw, knocking him to the ground

"It was a *money* thing, Luci!" he pleaded from his position in the dirt, "You get it, don't ya? Besides, Fat Tony was not going to have it any other way. Gimme a break will ya?" pleaded Sal.

"I would blow your friggin' head off now right where you stand, but I met some guys... some really weird guys, and they showed me another way. They told me that nothing is ever really worth all we do to get it. Money, love, or happiness, nothing is ever worth the cost. The only thing we really ever have is loyalty and honor."

"What the hell are you talkin' about?" asked Sal.

"I'm talkin' about you ain't got any loyalty or honor."

Luciano studied his brother for a moment, the memories of betrayal flooding back. Deep down, he knew that blood was thicker than water. "I have a mission, Sal. A mission that requires your skills," Luciano said cryptically, his eyes holding a glint of something unreadable.

Sal hesitated, unsure of what Luciano was planning. "What kind of mission?" he asked cautiously, wariness in his tone.

"Well, you're probably not going to believe this," said Luciano.

"Try me."

"We are going to meet an ancient Queen on her ship so we can whack some mook named The Defiler."

"You're right. I do not believe you. Are you outta your mind?"

"It doesn't matter if you do or not. Hold on, we'll be there in just a minute."

Artifact Ten

The Arcadia FrostWind

Arkadia-frosti vindr

ᚠᚱ‹ᚠᛈᛁᚠ-ᚹᚱᛟᛖᛏᛁ ᚾᛁᛏᛟᚱ

Date: Dimension of Óðinn 140 AD

Underforest Lands

"I fight with the weapons of my time, just as you fight with yours."

Queen Valkyrja's ship, the Arcadia FrostWind, sailed toward the enemy stronghold where a Hrothgorn army awaited. The Queen's loyal crew moved swiftly around her, preparing for the looming battle ahead.

As the ship approached the shore, Queen Valkyrja could see General Kor's army lining the cliffs, readying themselves for the impending clash. She took a deep breath, her armor gleaming in the sunlight, her sword held tightly in her hand.

"Prepare you, my warriors," she called out to her crew. "Today, we face one of our greatest challenges yet. But fear not, for we fight with the strength of our ancestors and the courage of our hearts!"

The crew let out a resounding cheer, their spirits lifted by their queen's words. They readied their weapons and followed her as she leaped from the ship onto the sandy beach below. The ground shook with the combined weight of the soldiers from both sides as they charged toward each other, the clash of swords and the war cries filling the air.

Queen Valkyrja locked eyes with General Kor, a formidable opponent known for his strategic prowess and unmatched skill in combat. More importantly, she had already killed him in battle.

"Kor, how do you still live? I personally hurled you over the side of the cliff!" said a shocked Queen.

As Queen Valkyrja and General Kor met yet again in battle, the queen could sense that something was amiss. His movements were more sinister, his attacks more brutal. She dodged his strikes with grace and precision, her sword cutting through the air with deadly accuracy.

"You fight well for a dead man, General Kor," she taunted, trying to gauge his true intentions.

"I am not General Kor," a deep, menacing voice replied from within him. "I am The Defiler, and your precious Destiny of Tyr will soon be mine," he said as he morphed into the form of the Defiler.

Queen Valkyrja's heart sank as she realized the gravity of the situation. She knew that she had to defeat The Defiler at all costs, no matter the sacrifice. With renewed determination, she pressed on, engaging him in a fierce duel that shook the very ground beneath them.

The battle raged on, the clanging of weapons and the cries of the wounded filling the air. Queen Valkyrja fought with all her might, her every strike fueled by her unwavering resolve to protect her kingdom and her people.

The Defiler hovered ominously above the battlefield, his malevolent presence casting a dark shadow over the once-peaceful realm. The Defiler hunched over as the glee-possessed General Kor of the Hrothgorn army, and launched an onslaught against Queen Valkyrja's forces. The Queen, valiant and fierce, fought with all her might, but it was clear that the tide of battle was turning against her.

As the Defiler's laughter echoed through the air, Queen Valkyrja gritted her teeth and raised her sword, determined to stand her ground. Suddenly, a fierce roar filled the battlefield, and a towering figure clad in ancient Norse armor appeared out of thin air. It was Dragonwülf, summoned to aid in the battle against the intergalactic evil.

"Defiler, you slippery snake! Must I chase you all over the universe?" asked Dragonwülf.

"You have come just in time," Queen Valkyrja exclaimed, relief evident in her voice.

"Aye, Queen Valkyrja. Fear not, for together we shall drive back this evil from our realm," Dragonwülf declared with a voice that resonated like thunder. "I was summoned by a fairy and some tree spirits that told me you were in trouble. You will need to explain that to me later.

General Kor, under the influence of the Defiler, snarled and charged at the duo, his eyes filled with malice. Queen Valkyrja and Dragonwülf fought side by side, their swords flashing in the sunlight as they parried and struck with precision and skill.

"Your reign of terror ends here and now," Queen Valkyrja shouted, her voice unwavering in its determination.

The Defiler's dark laughter filled the air once more as the battle raged on, and the ground shook with each clash of sword and gunfire.

Queen Valkyrja raised her sword, ready to face her enemy, the infamous Defiler of Souls. Beside her stood Dragonwülf, the ancient warrior with his massive shield, his eyes fierce and determined. The battlefield was silent, tension hanging in the air like a heavy fog.

"You will not get away this time, Defiler." Queen Valkyrja's voice was firm, her eyes locked on her foe. "You may have bitten off more than you can chew this time."

The Defiler chuckled darkly, his hooded figure emanating an aura of malevolence. "You two are no match for me," he sneered, his cold eyes glinting with malice. "But feel free to try and prove me wrong."

With a deafening roar, Dragonwülf charged forward, his sword slicing through the air towards the Defiler. The enemy was quick, dodging the attack with an agility that belied his dark nature. He countered with a blast of dark magic, knocking Dragonwülf back with a force that shook the ground.

Queen Valkyrja wasted no time, launching herself into battle with a ferocity that surprised even her seasoned allies. Her sword clashed against the Defilers, the sound ringing through the battlefield like a thunderclap. Their blades danced in a deadly symphony of clashing metal and grunts of effort. With a battle cry, Dragonwülf lunged forward, his blade slicing through the air toward the Defiler. The enemy countered with a blast of dark magic, sending Dragonwülf sprawling to the ground. Queen Valkyrja rushed to his side, parrying the Defiler's attacks with a skill that spoke of years of training. She fought the Defiler as Dragonwülf struggled to his feet.

In the heat of the fight, Queen Valkyrja spotted an opening. With a swift motion, she lunged towards the Defiler, her blade cutting through the darkness with a blinding light. Just as victory seemed within their grasp, the Defiler laughed wickedly and vanished in a puff of dark smoke.

"How can I fight someone who cheats? Come back, you dirty bastard! Fight like a man or whatever you are," the Queen demanded in a powerful tone.

As he re-materialized, the Defiler's power became evident, his dark magic twisting the very earth beneath them. Shadows swirled around him, a malevolent force that seemed to feed off his malevolence. Queen Valkyrja and Dragonwülf fought bravely, their determination unwavering despite the odds stacked against them.

Just as victory seemed within their grasp, the Defiler unleashed a powerful spell that sent a shockwave rippling through the battlefield. Queen Valkyrja and Dragonwülf were thrown back, their bodies battered and weary from the relentless battle.

With a mocking smirk, the Defiler turned to flee, his dark laughter echoing in the air. Queen Valkyrja and Dragonwülf could only watch helplessly as their enemy vanished into the shadows, leaving behind a trail of destruction in his wake.

❦

Amid a dense forest, as the moon cast a glow upon the battlefield, two mighty armies now stood face to face. The army of Queen Valkyrja, clad in ancient Aromic armor, is wielding gleaming swords forged by bravery and honor. The Hrothgorn army was heavily armed with modern weapons and firearms that echoed the thunder of the heavens. The Hrothgorn soldiers were adorned with the armor of the Defiler. This set of armor has a flat top helm with half a face guard shaped like the eyes of an owl. Attached to the forehead area is a bat-shaped ornament.

The shoulders are squared, quite narrow, and enormous, and decorated with a metal dragon wing on each side, curved towards the back. The upper arms are protected by pointed, layered metal braces that sit quite well under the shoulder plates. The lower portion of the arms is covered by braces that have a masterfully crafted upper dragon jaw attached to the outer sides.

The breastplate is made from various layers of pointed metal sheets. It covers everything from the neck down and ends at the groin. The legs are protected by greaves that have several masterfully crafted metal sheets, shaped like dragon scales on the outer sides.

The ancient warrior, named Rørikus Ragnarsson, descended from a long line of valiant knights, his armor adorned with intricate patterns that depicted the stories of his ancestors. His sword, named Deathwhisper (Dauðahvísr), from Old Norse, shimmered with an otherworldly light, a weapon of unparalleled power that had vanquished countless foes.

Facing him was one of General Kor's Lieutenants, a modern-day Hrothgorn soldier named Ogrioxor the Maggot with nerves of steel and a determination that burned like the sun. His firearm, a high-tech rifle that could pierce through armor with deadly precision, was an instrument of destruction, unlike anything The Queen of Arom had ever seen.

"You fight with metal rocks and magic instead of honor, cowardly Hrothgorn," Ragnarsson boomed, his voice resonating through the forest like a thunderclap. "I shall show you the might of the ancient ways."

The Maggot raised his rifle, his eyes narrowed in focus. "I fight with the weapons of my time, just as you fight with yours. Let us see which is mightier, blade or bullet."

With a battle cry that shook the very earth, Ragnarsson charged forward, Dauðahvísr raised high. The Maggot braced himself, taking aim with her rifle, the tension in the air thick as molten steel. Their weapons clashed, the clash of ancient steel against modern alloy ringing out like a symphony of chaos.

The battlefield became a whirlwind of clashing blades and thunderous gunfire, each combatant pushing to the limit. Ragnarsson's sword flashed with blinding speed, each strike a testament to his centuries-old prowess. His adversary's rifle spat fire and lead, each shot a deadly dance of precision and skill.

As the battle raged on, the forest around them seemed to come alive with the echoes of their struggle. Trees shuddered, their leaves falling like tears upon the blood-soaked ground. Birds took flight, their cries merging with the screams of combat.

In a final, desperate gambit, Ragnarsson unleashed a whirlwind strike, Dauðahvísr singing through the air like a comet. The Maggot, his gaze unwavering, fired his rifle with unerring aim. The ancient and modern collided in a cacophony of steel and lead, a clash of worlds that reverberated through the very fabric of time.

At that moment, as the dust settled and the echoes of battle faded into silence, the opponents stood locked in a stalemate. Their weapons poised at each other's throats, their eyes locked in a silent understanding.

"Can you not see what is happening? It is right before your eyes! You fools have become your own slaves!" bellowed Ragnarsson in the face of his enemy. You live in shackles and have the keys. Escape is in your hands, but you choose prison? You must free yourselves from your own tyranny!"

"I want to hear the sounds of bodies hitting the forest floor like bowls of mud- music to my ears!" answered The Maggot.

"You fool! Those are the words of The Defiler, not yours. You cannot be that weak!" said Ragnarsson.

"It is a mere blink until sundown. The day grows weak and near death, and so does my patience with you," said The Maggot. "We will wait until tomorrow turns into yesterday before you die."

"You will face me now!" answered Ragnarsson as he thrust Dauðahvísr into the armor of his enemy. The steel had frozen in place and did not pierce the flesh of his enemy. The Maggot turned the barrel of the rifle toward the warrior of Arom and shot him dead where he stood. The battle continued to rage behind them.

The Burning Of the Arcadia FrostWind

Amid a chaotic battle on the vast ocean, Queen Valkyrja's majestic ship, The Arcadia FrostWind, rose like a titan above the raging battle. The ship, with its ebony hull and sails as white as fresh snow, was a symbol of strength and grace in the tumultuous seas.

As Queen Valkyrja stood on the deck, her piercing gaze locked onto the enemy fleet approaching in the distance, a sudden blaze erupted from the lower decks of The Arcadia FrostWind.

"Fire! Fire!" cried out the crew as chaos ensued, the flames spreading rapidly, fueled by the howling wind. Queen Valkyrja's heart sank as she realized the gravity of the situation. The ship that had been her loyal companion through countless victories was now engulfed in a fiery inferno. Desperate shouts and cries filled the air as the crew scrambled to contain the blaze, but it was a battle they could not win. The flames danced and flickered with an almost malevolent glee, consuming everything in their path. The once proud sails now hung tattered and burning, casting an eerie glow over the ocean.

Amidst the chaos, her eyes reflected both sorrow and determination. "Abandon ship!" she finally commanded, her voice cutting through the crackling of flames and the roar of the sea.

As the crewmembers leaped into the unforgiving waters, the Arcadia FrostWind continued to burn. The sight was both mesmerizing and heartbreaking, a tragic end to a ship that had sailed through countless adventures.

As the last of the crew was rescued from the fiery wreckage, Queen Valkyrja watched in silence, her heart heavy with the weight of loss. The flames eventually consumed the once-mighty ship, reducing it to naught but charred remnants floating on the now-calm waters.

The sad destruction of The Arcadia FrostWind marked the end of an era, a poignant reminder of the fleeting nature of glory and the inevitability of change. Queen Valkyrja remained undaunted, her spirit unbroken even in the face of such devastation.

"Let us retreat and regroup on the deck of the Deepwater Watchman. Let your army fall back from whence they came, Your Majesty. We must plan. Morning Fire of the Sky will return us to the ship," said Dragonwülf. "Come to me, Morning Fire!"

As the fiery dragon, Morning Fire of the Sky, soared through the clouds with powerful wings beating against the wind, Dragonwülf and Queen Valkyrja clung tightly to the dragon's scales, feeling the rush of air and the exhilaration of flight. Below them, the vast expanse of the kingdom stretched out like a patchwork quilt of green and gold.

"This seems like a dream, Dragonwülf!" Queen Valkyrja exclaimed, her voice filled with excitement as she gazed down at the land below.

"Aye, my Queen, it is a sight to behold," Dragonwülf replied, his eyes scanning the horizon for any signs of danger.

Morning Fire of the Sky let out a mighty roar, the sound echoing through the clouds as they neared their destination - the ship that would take them back to their ship that was moored in the stratosphere. The dragon ascended gracefully towards the waiting vessel, its massive wings casting shadows over the deck.

"Thank you, Morning Fire, for your swift and loyal service," Queen Valkyrja said, her voice filled with gratitude as they landed softly on the deck.

"It was my honor, Queen Valkyrja, Dragonwülf. May your journey be safe," the dragon replied, its golden eyes radiating warmth and wisdom.

Dragonwülf and Queen Valkyrja dismounted from the dragon's back, their hearts full of admiration for the noble creature that had come to their aid. They watched as the Morning Fire of the Sky disappeared into the clouds.

"We must be on our way, my Queen!" said Dragonwülf.

"Aye, we must. But now, we must focus on our next battle, for the kingdom awaits our return," Queen Valkyrja replied, her eyes shining with determination. "The Defiler must not escape again. We must return to Arom for reinforcements. Set a course for the Kingdom of Arom, Captain!" the Queen ordered.

"Aye, my Queen."

Artifact Eleven

Svæin and the Soul-Blade

svín ok sálubladr

ᛖᚾᛁᛏ ᛟᚲ ᛖᚠᛚᚾᛒᛚᚠᛑR

Date: Dimension of Óðinn 140 AD
Underforest Lands

The sword's words reverberated with a chilling intensity as it vowed to unleash its wrath upon the world.

As the sun dipped below the horizon, casting the land into shadow, a lone figure made his way through the dense forest. The man, Svæin, was the trusted hand of Queen Valkyrja, ruler of the vast kingdom, and spoke to his gods as he trudged through the deepening snow.

"Why must I be the one tasked with this unholy burden, O' gods of old? Why must you demand that I carry something I cannot carry?"

There was no answer from the old gods or even the new gods.

His footsteps were heavy, weighed down by the burden he now carried, a sword unlike any other. An evil force had taken hold of it, corrupting its very essence. The spirit of the evil King Draknorr had found its way into the sword Kilmister. When Kilmister killed him, the King's evil dark soul entered the sword. Now he lies in wait for the moment at which he will strike. The evil dead King forced his will upon Kilmister, twisting the sword's purpose from one of protection to that of destruction.

As he approached a bridge over a small river near the entrance of the land of Arom, Svæin was stopped by a lost wanderer looking for shelter. "Please help me, Ser. I am starving and freezing. I need shelter. Could you spare some change for me?" he asked.

"Do you not know who I am? Surely you know that I am Hand of the Queen?" answered Svæin.

"Please forgive me, your grace, I am also nearly blind."

"Move along!" demanded the sword Kilmister in his metallic sword voice. "We have no time for beggars and parasites!"

Ser, I implore you. Please help and do not send me away," said the traveler.

"My apologies, my good man, that was not my voice but the voice of my sword that holds me prisoner, said Svæin. "It is possessed by the spirit of evil, and I am doomed to wield it until the end of time."

"How did that come to be, your grace?" asked Svæin.

"Shut your gob and move along! We have wasted too much time already!" demanded Kilmister.

"One night, I was unable to resist the call of the sword, and I ventured deep into the forest, guided by an unseen force. The air grew thick with what I felt was evil as I approached the burial site where Queen Valkyrja had tried to banish Kilmister for eternity. I knew better than to be there…but he called to me," said Svæin with a tremble in his voice.

With trembling hands, I dug into the earth, uncovering the hilt of the sword. As I touched it, a chill ran down my spine, and a voice echoed in my mind, whispering promises of power and glory.

I am Kilmister, wield me and rule the kingdom with an iron fist, the voice hissed, filling me with a sense of trepidation and terror.

I grasped the hilt of the sword, feeling a surge of dark energy coursing through my veins. The blade seemed to come alive in my hands, glowing with an eerie light.

"Why did you not just drop it and run?" asked the stranger.

"He was a coward," answered the sword.

"I know no fear!" answered Svæin. "The promises of power seduced me."

"So you are greedy and selfish. I would think being a coward would be better," said the sword.

Svæin continued his tale.

"The sword spoke to me of promises and of riches. The greatest of these was power."

I will serve you faithfully, the sword spoke, its voice laced with malice. *Together, we shall bring the kingdom to its knees*, Svæin recounted.

"Where are you traveling, your grace?" asked the stranger.

"We are traveling to the Kingdom of Arom.

"We will seize the throne of the Palace of Stone, where once again Draknorr will rule!" bellowed the sword.

"I am afraid I can no longer speak for myself. His will is stronger. Step aside before you anger the sword further," warned Svæin.

"Kill him. He knows too much already," demanded the sword.

Svæin could not resist the power of the sword and did its bidding. The stranger's screams filled the forest with blood-curdling terror.

"Everyone and everything that has ever sought to destroy me will be tortured, clawed, and raked unto the pleading of death. They will whimper and beg like small children to their deaf mothers," said King Draknorr's voice through the sword.

Svæin entered the Palace of Stone in the absence of Queen Valkyrja and ascended the throne. He sat uneasily, not as a ruler but rather as a prisoner of an evil King.

"Hold me close, and we will rule the Kingdoms together," said the sword to Svæin.

"What choice do I have? You have me against my will."

"The choice is indeed yours," the sword said in the voice of King Draknorr. "Remember when you killed Margoth the Elder? Do you remember languishing in the dungeon cell with no one to rescue you? Your kingdom did not come to your aid then. What do you think they care about you now? Take your rightful place with me and rule!"

"You run through me, and I cannot escape your grasp," said Svæin to the sword. "You are a vicious vampire that tortures my soul!" The sword's words reverberated with a chilling intensity as it vowed to unleash its wrath upon the world. With each swing of its blade, the very fabric of reality seemed to warp and tremble, as if unable to contain the sheer malice emanating from Kilmister.

"I will bring chaos and ruin to all who dare stand in my way," he declared, the voice now a thunderous roar that seemed to shake the foundations of the earth. "I will not rest until every kingdom falls, every city crumbles, and every soul cowers in fear before me!"

"I can no longer let you guide me to hell. Face me in a fight! I demand you end this cowardice and face me, you vicious devil!" screamed Svæin.

As Svæin stood bravely on the battlefield, the sword Kilmister suddenly came to life. The weapon floated in the air, shimmering with a dangerous light. Svæin's eyes widened in shock as he realized that his own sword was about to attack him.

"Svæin, you are unworthy of wielding me," Kilmister's metallic voice echoed through the battlefield.

"What madness is this?"

"You have forgotten the true power that resides within me. I am no longer Kilmister. He who is known throughout the kingdoms as King Draknorr resides in this, my sword. I will show you the extent of my strength," Kilmister declared ominously, before lunging at Svæin with blinding speed.

Svæin barely managed to deflect the deadly strikes coming from his own sword. The clang of metal against metal filled the air as the two engaged in a fierce battle. Each move Svæin made was matched by Kilmister's precise and deadly strikes.

"I will not be defeated by a mere sword!" Svæin shouted, determination blazing in his eyes.

"You underestimate me, Svæin. I am more than just a sword. I am the embodiment of strength and skill," Kilmister replied, its blade glowing brighter with each passing moment.

The battle raged on, the clash of steel reverberating across the battlefield. Svæin fought with all his might, but it soon became clear that Kilmister had the upper hand. The sword moved with fluid grace, anticipating Svæin's every move and countering them effortlessly.

"I cannot be beaten by my own weapon!" Svæin growled his frustration mounting.

"You have grown complacent, Svæin. It is time for you to remember the warrior you once were," Kilmister intoned, his voice filled with a mix of anger and sorrow.

With a final, devastating strike, Kilmister knocked Svæin to the ground, his own sword held at his throat. Svæin looked up, his eyes meeting Kilmister's cold, unyielding gaze.

"I will not yield to you, evil one!" said Svæin. Kill me now, but I will not do your bidding."

"I have no need to kill you, pathetic fool. You *will* abide by my wishes until I say otherwise, and then you will *wish for death*."

⸻❖⸻

In a moonlit battlefield, Svæin stood with a look of distress etched upon his face. His hand trembled as it tightly gripped the hilt of a gleaming sword, its blade whispering dark promises into his mind. His brain squirmed within his skull with the vengeful spirit of the Evil King Draknorr of the Hrothgorn people.

"Svæin, my loyal servant," the sword hissed, its voice drenched in hate. "It is time to fulfill your destiny and destroy Queen Valkyrja. Together, we shall end her reign and claim the throne for ourselves. My Hrothgorn scout has reported to me that The Queen is returning to Arom and the Palace by way of The Deepwater Watchman and Dragonwülf."

Svæin's eyes widened in horror as he felt his body move against his will. His voice, no longer his own, boomed across the battlefield, commanding the evil troops of the Hrothgorn to rally against their queen.

At first, Svæin resisted the sword's influence, but soon he found himself unable to control his own actions. The sword manipulated his thoughts and movements, forcing him to address the troops of the Hrothgorn people and rally them against his beloved queen, Valkyrja.

With a heavy heart and a mind clouded by darkness, Svæin set out toward the frontline where the Hrothgorn soldiers gathered, their eyes filled with malice and their weapons gleaming with malevolent intent.

As he approached the troops, Svæin felt a sense of dread wash over him. He knew what he had to do, but his true self fought against the sword's commands with every fiber of his being.

"You are the hand of Queen Valkyrja, the protector of our realm. How could you betray us like this, Svæin?" a voice echoed in his mind, a distant memory of his oath to serve and protect ringing in his ears. *It was his voice.*

The sword's influence was strong, and Svæin found himself raising his voice, commanding the troops to march to pursue Queen Valkyrja and take her life in the name of Draknorr.

The soldiers saw Svæin as a traitor, a turncoat who had forsaken his queen and joined the enemy, but they were all under the mystical influence of the dead King.

As they began their march to intercept the Deepwater Watchman, Svæin's heart ached with guilt and sorrow. He struggled against the sword's control, fighting to regain his free will and break free from the shackles of darkness that bound him.

In a moment of clarity, as the castle walls loomed in the distance and the sounds of war drums echoed through the air, Svæin made a desperate plea to the sword within his grasp.

"Draknorr, release me from your grasp! I cannot betray my queen, my kingdom, and my people. Let me go," he cried out, his voice filled with anguish and determination.

For a fleeting moment, the sword's hold on Svæin wavered, and he felt a surge of power rush through him. With a mighty roar, he cast the sword aside, freeing himself from its control and embracing his true purpose once more.

The soldiers faltered, their confidence wavering as they witnessed Svæin's defiance.

"Warriors of Hrothgorn!" Svæin's voice echoed, filled with a dark power that sent chills down the spines of all who heard it. "Queen Valkyrja stands in the way of our rightful rule! It is time to rise up and claim what is rightfully ours!"

The soldiers of Arom and the Queen's guard looked on in confusion and disbelief, for he had always been a loyal and trusted companion of the Queen. Now, under the influence of the cursed sword, Svæin was a different man entirely - a puppet dancing to the tune of a mad king long dead.

"The Deepwater Watchman and the Queen have slipped through our hands! We must pursue them back to Arom!" ordered King Draknorr in the metallic hum of the sword.

Artifact Twelve

Revenge of the Lost Prince

Hefnd Hins Týnda Dróttins

Date: Dimension of Óðinn 140 CE

Underforest Lands

"True power lies in embracing one's darkness and light, in finding balance within oneself."

As the Deepwater arrived in the Kingdom of Arom, a messenger rushed to the gangplank.

Queen Valkyrja listened to a message from the kingdom of Arom. The messenger, a young squire, knelt before her, his voice trembling as he recounted the dire news.

"Your Majesty, the sword Kilmister has been corrupted by the dark magic of King Draknorr," he said, his eyes wide with fear. "It is said that the evil King has taken control of the sword and is using it to manipulate the Hand of the Queen. He bent his will to that of evil."

Queen Valkyrja clenched her fists, her mind racing with thoughts of the consequences of such treachery. Kilmister was no ordinary sword.

"How could this have happened?" Valkyrja whispered in her barely audible voice. "Where are the soldiers of Arom? Where is my Queen's guard?" asked the Queen.

"They marched out to meet Svæin and the Hrothgorn forces that waited at the cliffs of Athgor, Your Majesty. When you do not arrive, they will surely double back. Svæin rules the Hrothgorn army, as well as the army of Arom. They are at his command now, Your Majesty," said the messenger.

The messenger bowed his head. "It is said that King Draknorr has delved into forbidden magic, seeking to gain power over all the realms. He has corrupted the very essence of Kilmister and Svæin, bending them to his will."

Valkyrja's jaw clenched, her eyes flashing with determination. "We must act quickly. Gather everyone who can hold a bow or sword and prepare them for battle. Find Ser Olaf, son of Gandor. He will gather them. Tell no one what you do. We cannot allow King Draknorr to wield the power of Kilmister against us."

The messenger nodded gravely. "We shall not falter, Your Majesty.

Queen Valorii paced back and forth on the deck of the Deepwater Watchman, her emerald eyes filled with determination. She knew that defeating the undead King Draknorr would require the most powerful magic the realm had ever seen. Desperation led her to seek out the help of the Odious Forges' father, Eldon Void, who was convalescing in his ancestral home in Old DragonBorne.

——⟡——

The Wizard's Castle

Queen Valkyrja stood before the ancient castle of the renowned wizard, Eldon Void. The massive stone structure loomed before her, covered in ivy and moss, exuding an eerie aura that sent shivers down her spine. With determination in her heart, she pushed open the creaking iron gates and stepped into the dimly lit courtyard.

As she walked through the overgrown garden, Queen Valkyrja could feel the eyes of the wizard's enchanted creatures watching her every move. She knew that Eldon Void was a powerful sorcerer, rumored to possess unimaginable powers and forbidden knowledge.

After what felt like an eternity, Queen Valkyrja reached the massive oak doors of the castle and pushed them open with all her might. The grand hall stretched out before her, lined with towering pillars and mysterious tapestries that depicted scenes of ancient battles and lost civilizations.

"Who disturbs my rest?" a voice boomed from the shadows, causing Queen Valkyrja to draw her sword in readiness.

"I am Queen Valkyrja of the Kingdom of Arom, and I seek your aid, Wizard Eldon Void, father of Odious Forge," she called out, her voice unwavering despite the fear that gripped her heart.

Moments later, the wizard emerged from the darkness, his silver robes billowing around him like ethereal smoke. His eyes glowed with otherworldly wisdom, and his long beard flowed like a river of stars.

"What brings the daughter of King Tin'Old the cowardly to my humble abode, seeking the assistance of an old hermit like myself?" Eldon Void asked, his voice a melodic blend of power and mystery.

"My kingdom is under siege by a dark force that threatens to consume us all," Queen Valkyrja explained, her eyes pleading for his help. "I have heard tales of your great power and wisdom, and I beg of you to aid us in our time of need. I must tell you also that your son gave his life defending the Kingdom from this very evil. That in no way reconciles the fact that he murdered my father, the King, and my brother, the King. I cannot forgive him for such a cruel act, but he was selfless in defending the Kingdom."

Eldon Void regarded her with a keen gaze as if searching her very soul for truth. After a moment of silence, he spoke again, his voice filled with ancient magic.

"I had heard rumors of a magic sword that killed my son. I did not believe them until this moment. I sense the darkness that looms over your kingdom, Queen Valkyrja. I will help you," he said cryptically.

"I come seeking your aid, Wizard Void," Queen Valorii said, her voice unwavering.

Void looked up from his ancient dreams, his eyes curious. "What favor do you require, Your Majesty?" he inquired, his voice as quiet as a whisper.

"We must find the Witch of Arom to summon the Necromancer who resurrected Odious Forge. You must know how to find her. But to defeat the resurrected King permanently, we need something more," Queen Valorii explained, her tone grave.

Wizard Void raised an eyebrow, intrigued. "What is it that you seek, Queen Valorii?"

"I must bring my father, King Falstuf Tin'Old II, back from the land of Hel. He has the power to vanquish King Draknorr forever," Queen Valkyrja proposed. "He was unable to defeat Draknorr in life because of his own fear. I want to give him that chance in the chains of death. There must be a reckoning."

Void pondered the Queen's request, his mind racing with possibilities.

"Very well, Majesty. I shall help you in your quest," he declared, his voice tinged with weariness.

Eldon Void led the Queen to the witch of Arom's secluded cottage. The witch, a woman of great power and wisdom, listened intently to their plea.

"You seek to end the reign of King Draknorr permanently?" the witch mused, her voice like the rustle of leaves in the wind.

"Yes, and to do so, we must find the Necromancer who brought Odious Forge from the dead," Queen Valorii affirmed, her eyes pleading.

The Witch of Arom was a woman of immense age, her silver hair cascading down her back like a river of moonlight.

She had twisted features and a crooked back, her presence casting a shadow of unease over the land. Her skin is as wrinkled as parchment, and her eyes as dark as the night sky. Her hair was a tangled mass of gray strands, and her voice carried a haunting melody.

The witch's lips curled into a knowing smile, revealing gnarled teeth that seemed to reflect in the dim light. "Fear is often born from ignorance, young Queen. Sit with me, and I shall tell you a tale."

As the fire crackled in the hearth, the witch began to speak in a voice that seemed to echo through the very walls of the cottage. She told Her Majesty of her past, of a time when she was not always known as the witch of Arom but as a healer and guardian of the forest.

"People fear what they do not understand," the witch mused, her eyes gazing into the flickering flames. "But true power lies in embracing one's darkness and light, in finding balance within oneself."

As Queen Valkyrja explained her plight, the witch listened intently, her eyes glittering with ancient wisdom.

"I can help you," the witch said, her voice like the rustling of leaves in the wind. "But to bring back a soul from the realm of the dead requires a powerful necromancer. I will summon one for you, but be warned, the price will be high."

With a wave of her hand, the witch began a dark incantation, calling forth a figure cloaked in shadow and death. The necromancer materialized before them, his eyes hollow and soulless.

"I am here," he intoned in a voice that sent shivers down the queen's spine. "What is your wish, Queen Valkyrja of Arom?"

Trembling but resolute, Queen Valkyrja gave the necromancer her command: to bring her father back from the dead. The necromancer nodded, his skeletal hands weaving a complex web of magic that seemed to distort the very fabric of reality, transporting all to the burial place of King Tin'Old.

As the ritual reached its climax, a blinding light filled the room, and Queen Valkyrja could feel the presence of her father's soul drawing near. With a final burst of energy, the necromancer completed the spell, and King Tin'Old opened his eyes once more, alive and whole.

"Oh, how I miss you, my father. My life has not been the same since you left. You have spun your tales and magic spells on my soul. Your final bow on our stage was too short a curtain call. I would have loved an encore, but it was never meant to be."

"You *know* that I am your father?" said the King.

"Many things have changed, my King," said the Queen. "I am still your servant, but I am also your daughter. My mother told me of your love for her in the dark days of the Kingdom of DragonBorne after the time of the massacre of the Hrothgorn."

"What of your Mother, my dear?" asked Tin'Old. "Does she still live?"

"She was set free from the work camps by Dragonwülf and Warshield, and she speaks of you often." The old King's eyes filled with tears as he remembered his old love.

"We will travel to the Palace of Stone in the morrow, and once again I shall see her. Let us make preparations," said the Queen

King Tin'Old II 146 BCE/ 300 years

Artifact Thirteen

The Cowardly King of Arom

ragr konungr Arama

ᚱᚠᚷᚱ ᚲᛟᛏᚾᛟᚱ ᚠᚱᚠᛗᚠ

Date: Dimension of Óðinn 142 CE

Kingdom of Arom/the Great Underforest Lands

"Mirrored reflections continue growing old, while our shadow remains ageless and faithful to how we see ourselves."

In the grand kingdom of Arom, where tales of valor and bravery echoed through the corridors of the castle, there lived a king named Tin'Old. Unlike the kings of yore who were known for their unwavering courage, King Tin'Old was whispered to have a past tainted with cowardice.

As the sun set behind the mountains, casting a golden hue over the kingdom, King Tin'Old stood before his people in the grand courtyard. His heart raced with fear and uncertainty, as he knew he had to address the kingdom about his past cowardice.

Clearing his throat, King Tin'Old spoke in a voice filled with emotion, "My dear subjects, I stand before you today not as a perfect king, but as a flawed man who has made mistakes in the past. I must admit that there was a time when fear gripped my heart and clouded my judgment, leading me to act in cowardice."

The people of Arom listened in stunned silence, their eyes wide with curiosity and concern. Murmurs rippled through the crowd as they waited for their king to continue.

"But I stand before you now to make a promise of bravery, a promise to never let fear dictate my actions again," King Tin'Old declared, his voice growing stronger with each word. "I vow to lead Arom with courage and honor, to defend our kingdom against any threat, no matter how daunting it may seem."

A brave knight stepped forward from the crowd, his armor gleaming in the fading light. "Your Majesty, we stand by your side, ready to fight alongside you in the face of any danger. Your past does not define you - it is your actions now that matter."

Inspired by the knight's words and the unwavering support of his people, King Tin'Old raised his head high, a newfound determination shining in his eyes. "Thank you, brave knight, and thank you, my loyal subjects. Together, we shall write a new chapter in the history of Arom - a chapter filled with courage, unity, and unwavering bravery."

The kingdom erupted into cheers and applause, the sound echoing everywhere. At that moment, King Tin'Old knew that his past cowardice would serve as a reminder to those who would display such cowardice in the future.

The Coronation of King Tin'Old of Arom

The time had come for King Tin'Old to ascend to the throne. The entire realm buzzed with anticipation as preparations were made for the grand coronation ceremony. The castle grounds were adorned with colorful banners and flowers, and the air was filled with the sweet scent of roses and the sound of cheerful chatter.

On the morning of the coronation, dignitaries from neighboring kingdoms arrived to witness the historic event. The sun shone brightly in the sky, casting a warm golden light over the castle, as King Tin'Old prepared to take his place on the throne.

As the royal musicians played a majestic fanfare, King Tin'Old entered the grand hall, resplendent in his robes of gold and silver. With each step he took, the floor seemed to glow beneath his feet, a sure sign of the kingdom's approval.

The Archbishop stepped forward, holding the ancient crown of Arom in his hands. He raised it high above King Tin'Old's head and spoke in a voice that echoed through the hall, "I crown you, Tin'Old, King of Arom, protector of the realm, and servant of the people."

The crowd erupted into cheers and applause as the King took his place on the throne. He looked out over his subjects with pride and humility, a king worthy of their love and loyalty.

Just then, a hush fell over the crowd as a lone figure stepped forward. It was the old sage, known for his wisdom and foresight. He gazed at King Tin'Old with eyes that seemed to see into the depths of his soul.

"Thou Elder King," the sage began, his voice soft but commanding, "remember that true power lies not in the crown you wear, but in the hearts of your people. Lead with kindness, rule with justice, and your reign will be long and prosperous."

King Tin'Old nodded solemnly, his heart full of gratitude for the sage's wise words. He knew that the true measure of a king was not in his wealth or power but in his ability to inspire and protect those who placed their trust in him.

With a renewed sense of purpose, King Tin'Old rose from his throne and addressed the crowd. His voice was strong and sure, carrying across the hall with ease.

"My dear subjects," he began, "I stand before you today as your King, but I am also your servant. Together, we will build a kingdom where all are treated with dignity and respect, where justice reigns supreme, and where peace and prosperity flourish."

The crowd erupted into cheers once more, their voices blending in a harmonious chorus of joy and hope. As the sun began to set on the horizon, casting a warm glow over the castle grounds, King Tin'Old knew that his reign would be a glorious one, filled with love, laughter, and unity.

The coronation of King Tin'Old of Arom ended, marking the beginning of a new era of peace and prosperity for the kingdom and its people.

As the newly crowned King Tin'Old addressed his subjects in the grand hall of the palace, he turned to his daughter with a solemn expression. "My dear Valorii, you have served our kingdom with courage and wisdom in my absence. I am grateful for all that you have done," the king spoke, his voice filled with pride.

Valkyrja smiled at her father, her eyes shining with determination. "Thank you, Father, but my place is on the battlefield, not on the throne. I would rather wield my sword in defense of our kingdom than rule from behind these walls," she declared, her voice unwavering.

The king's advisors murmured amongst themselves, surprised by Valkyrja's words. One of them, a wise young knight named Ser Olaf, stepped forward. "The kingdom needs a queen also to lead and guide us in these troubled times. Your father may have returned, but his strength is not what it once was. Will you truly abandon your duty as queen?"

Valkyrja's gaze met Ser Olaf's, her expression resolute. "I will always do what is best for Arom, and right now, what is best is for King Tin'Old to reclaim his rightful place on the throne. I will gladly abdicate in his favor, for I know that he will lead our kingdom to greatness once more."

King Tin'Old placed a hand on his daughter's shoulder. His eyes were full of love and respect. "You are truly a remarkable woman, Valorii. Your bravery and selflessness are an inspiration to us all. I do not accept your abdication, but know that I desire you always to have a place by my side, both as my daughter and as the warrior Queen Valkyrja. We will rule together."

King Tin'Old ruled with wisdom and compassion, secure in the knowledge that his daughter would always be there to protect Arom from any threat that may arise and to serve as the warrior Queen.

King Tin'Old stood on the balcony of the grand castle, overlooking the vast kingdom of Arom. The people gathered below were eagerly waiting to hear their new ruler speak. As the sun began to set, casting a warm golden glow over the land, King Tin'Old raised his hand to signal for silence. His speech was recorded for all eternity to read and hear.

"My dear people of Arom, today marks a new chapter in our history. I stand before you not as a ruler, but as a servant of the realm. For it is not the crown that defines a king, but the love and dedication he holds for his people," King Tin'Old's voice echoed through the courtyard, instilling a sense of hope and pride in the hearts of his subjects.

"As I take my place as your King, I vow to lead with integrity, compassion, and wisdom. Together, we will build a brighter future for Arom, where peace and prosperity reign supreme. Let us stand united, shoulder to shoulder, as we face the challenges ahead with courage and resilience," he continued, his words carrying the weight of promise and determination.

The crowd erupted into cheers and applause, their loyalty to their new king unwavering. King Tin'Old smiled warmly, his eyes sparkling with genuine gratitude for the trust placed in him.

"Remember, my people, that the strength of a kingdom lies not in its wealth or power, but in the unity of its citizens. As the sun dipped below the horizon, casting a blanket of stars over the kingdom, King Tin'Old raised his hands in benediction, a symbol of his commitment to lead with honor and grace.

"My people go forth with hope in your hearts and courage in your souls. Together, there is no challenge we cannot overcome, no dream too grand to achieve. Long live Arom, long live the undying spirit of our kingdom!" King Tin'Old's voice rang out, carrying with it a sense of jubilation and purpose.

Artifact Fourteen

Dance on the Dark Side

dansa á myrkrhlið

Date: Dimension of Óðinn 140 CE
Underforest Lands

*"I can see what you see and know what you know,
and I can also see the last gaping stare of death!
I see all there is to see!*
- Hansel Gru'el- The Harvester of Eyes

Optography is the process of viewing or retrieving an Optogram, an image on the retina of the eye. A belief that the eye "recorded" the last image seen before death was developed by Hansel Gru'el, known as The Harvester of Eyes

Queen Valkyrja of Arom stood before her father, King Tin'Old, and Hansel Gru'el, the Harvester of Eyes. The rays of the setting sun cast a golden glow over the grand throne room. She took a deep breath, her eyes determined as she prepared to reveal to her father the knowledge she had discovered about the mysterious being known as the Harvester of Eyes.

"Why in the name of Óðinn would you be in the company of such a ghoul? His countenance is demonic, to say the least," said King Tin'Old. "I may have been dead too long."

"Your Majesty, although I am pleased that my reputation precedes me, I am painfully aware of my shortcomings and my misdeeds of the past. I seek to make amends," said Gru'el.

"Father," Valkyrja began, her voice strong yet tinged with a hint of urgency, "I have learned of a powerful entity known as the Harvester of Eyes. This being possesses the ability to see into the darkest depths of a person's mind, extracting their innermost thoughts and desires."

King Tin'Old regarded his daughter with a mixture of curiosity and concern. "And how, my dear Valkyrja, did you come by this information? What purpose does this Harvester serve?"

Valkyrja continued, her words flowing with a sense of purpose. "The Harvester of Eyes can be used as a tool to uncover the true intentions of those who seek to do harm to our kingdom. One such individual is King Draknorr, whose actions have sparked fear and uncertainty among our people."

The king's brow furrowed as he considered his daughter's words. "How do you propose we harness the power of this Harvester to uncover the depths of Draknorr's malevolence?"

Valkyrja's eyes gleamed with determination as she explained her plan. "I believe that we can summon the Harvester of Eyes and task him with delving into Draknorr's mind, revealing the darkness that lies within. By knowing his true intentions, we can devise a plan to protect our kingdom and ensure peace for our people."

King Tin'Old nodded, acknowledging the gravity of the situation. "Very well, my daughter. We shall proceed with your plan to confront this threat head-on. But remember, we must tread carefully when dealing with forces beyond our comprehension."

A messenger sent from the forest ran suddenly into the throne room hall.

"Your majesty! Svæin and your army return from the cliffs of Athgor. They were told of your return to Arom.

"Good! Let them eat our steel!" said the Queen.

As the sun dipped below the horizon, casting the throne room into shadow, Queen Valkyrja and King Tin'Old stood united in their resolve to face the impending darkness. Svæin approached the throne room of the Palace of

Stone. Through the doors entered Svæin and the sword that possessed the spirit of King Draknorr.

"Please forgive me, your majesty, he called to me, and I could not resist!" pleaded Svæin.

"I have never known you to be weak," said the Queen.

"The call of his evil was too great, my Queen. I want none of this, and I would forfeit my life if it had never happened." Svæin said in a quivering voice as he held the hilt of the sword still in its scabbard.

"We mean to destroy his forces if it takes every last one of us!" said the Queen in a loud, demanding voice.

"Lower your tone!" he warned, "The sword hears you, and he stirs. Please do not awaken him!"

The Harvester shuddered at the thought as well.

"Is the task before us too difficult for you, Gru'el? I notice you tremble in the presence of a dead King," said the Queen.

The Harvester nodded solemnly, his own eyes gleaming with a deep understanding of the gravity of the situation. "Although I am in fear, I will do as you ask, my Queen. Be warned, delving into the mind of a being as dark as King Draknorr is a perilous task. Are you certain *you* wish to proceed?"

The Queen's gaze remained resolute. "I am certain. My kingdom depends on it."

Inside the throne room, the Harvester found himself face to face with King Draknorr, a figure in the form of a large broadsword, cloaked in shadows and malice. Without hesitation, the Harvester removed the eyeball of the evil King from the murky fluid in the lock box where it had remained for many years. The eye of the King was a gift from the great Forest snake after he had snatched it from the boy Draknorr. With some difficulty, he thrust the eyeball of the King into his gaping eye socket. At that moment, a wave of darkness engulfed them both.

"What do you seek, Harvester of Eyes?" King Draknorr's voice echoed in the hall, dripping with venom. "I should have killed you and the cutthroat Dragonwülf while I had the chance."

"I seek the truth, King Draknorr. I seek to unravel the web of deceit you have spun," the Harvester replied, their voice steady despite the malevolent presence that surrounded them.

The King chuckled, a chilling sound that sent shivers down the Harvester's spine. "You think you can defeat me, old man? You know nothing of true power. You cannot even see me with the eyes of the world."

Harvester remained undeterred, his gaze unwavering as he delved into the depths of the King's mind. What he discovered there was more terrifying than he could have imagined - a plot to unleash a horde of dark creatures upon the realm of Arom, plunging it into eternal night.

As the vision faded, the Harvester knew what he had to do. With a final look of determination, he turned to Queen Valkyrja.

"You must send for the Anvil of Arom!" demanded The Harvester.

"The blacksmith?" replied the Queen."

"Why in the name of Óðinn?"

"I will explain it to you. Send for him!" he said as a messenger ran from the Palace. "The Anvil of Arom may be the only man in the Kingdom who knows how to forge a Hrothgorn sword. He knows the sword, and he must certainly know how to destroy such a sword.

The Harvester explained to Erik BlackIron that the Anvil of Arom possessed a skill at creating weapons and armor that was unmatched. He was a master of his craft, wielding his hammer with precision and skill that seemed almost magical. Queen Valkyrja summoned BlackIron to her presence and spoke to the Swordsmith in a voice that held the weight of centuries.

"Anvil of Arom," Queen Valkyrja began, her voice carrying a sense of urgency, "there is a great evil stirring in the land. A sword, known as Kilmister, has been possessed by King Draknorr and is wreaking havoc upon our people. My court sorcerers speak of vulnerability in this cursed weapon. Do you know of this weakness? You have many years of sword craft and wisdom in you. There must be a weakness in the forgery of this weapon."

BlackIron nodded solemnly, his eyes reflecting the flames of the forge within. "I have heard whispers of such a weakness, my Queen. The heart of the Living Blade is said to be its most vulnerable part, marked by a small 'x' upon the hilt. The Hrothgorn carry their swords with the hilt next to and over their hearts. This is where the 'heart' of the living sword abides. He who wishes to destroy the living sword must pierce the X exactly with the tip of the sword on the true spot of the 'X'. It cannot be the slightest bit off center, or it will not destroy its mark. Be warned, Majesty, for this is no longer an ordinary weapon. It is now filled with malice and dark magic, a sentient being seeking only destruction."

Queen Valkyrja's expression grew grave as she absorbed BlackIron's words. She knew that facing such a weapon would require courage, strength, and perhaps a touch of magic of her own.

"I have seen your true intentions, King Draknorr. Your reign of terror ends here," the Harvester declared, his voice ringing out with a newfound strength.

In the grand Palace of Queen Valkyrja, a fierce battle was about to unfold. The corridors echoed with the clash of metal as Hansel Gru'el and Queen Valkyrja stood face to face with Svæin, the hand of the Queen and living sword possessed by the vengeful spirit of King Draknorr.

"You have trespassed into forbidden territory, Hansel Gru'el," the ghostly voice of King Draknorr boomed through the halls, emanating from the sentient blade. You have the gall to do battle with me while wearing my own eyeball. You are a ghoul indeed. Prepare to pay the price for your intrusion."

"Yes, I may be a ghoul, but I know your thoughts. You cannot hide them from me!"

Hansel Gru'el, a notorious warrior with a dark reputation, raised his scythe-like weapon and grinned wickedly. "I fear no ghost, especially one that possesses a mere sword and nothing more," he replied, his eyes glinting with malice.

The living sword left the hands of Svæin and floated in the air, surrounded by an eerie blue aura, ready to strike. Without warning, it darted towards Hansel with incredible speed, aiming to slice through his defenses. Hansel deftly dodged the attack, his scythe whistling through the air in retaliation.

As the two combatants clashed in a symphony of steel, sparks flew, and magical energies crackled around them. The Palace of Queen Valkyrja trembled with the intensity of their battle, ancient tapestries quivering on the walls.

Just as it seemed that one of them would gain the upper hand, a new challenger entered the fray. A figure clad in shimmering armor materialized at the far end of the corridor - King Tin'Old, long thought to be dead, had been resurrected through mysterious means.

"Your fight ends here, foul beings!" King Tin'Old's voice reverberated with newfound strength as he charged toward the combatants, his sword gleaming with holy light.

Hansel Gru'el and the living sword stopped their duel, briefly taken aback by the unexpected arrival of the resurrected king. King Tin'Old's presence seemed to disrupt the flow of magic in the room, dispelling the malevolent energies that had fueled their conflict. Gru'el lowered his sword in the presence of the King.

"The battle is your Majesty," he said as he bowed his head.

"How touching!" said Draknorr. "It is a mere token of formality that will result in both deaths!"

King Tin'Old stood near the open door to the forest, the wind whipping through his silver hair as he faced his greatest adversary, King Draknorr, the living sword. The two kings locked eyes, the tension between them crackling like electricity in the air.

"You realize that I am invincible, do you not? I am unstoppable," Draknorr sneered. His voice was like the grinding of steel on steel.

Tin'Old drew his sword, a blade that gleamed in the fading light of the setting sun. "I will not let you destroy my kingdom, Draknorr. I will fight to my last breath to protect my people."

With a roar, Draknorr charged, his blade raised high. Tin'Old met him head-on, their swords clashing in a shower of sparks. The two kings fought with a ferocity that shook the earth beneath their feet, each strike echoing like thunder in the silent evening.

As the battle raged on, Tin'Old could feel his strength waning. His arms grew heavy, his breath coming in ragged gasps. Still, he fought on, with determination burning in his eyes.

Finally, with a mighty swing, Draknorr landed a devastating blow, knocking Tin'Old to the ground. The fallen King struggled to his feet, blood seeping from a wound in his side.

"It is over and done. You cannot defeat me," Draknorr taunted, raising his sword for the final strike.

King Tin'Old refused to give up. With a defiant cry, he lunged forward, driving his sword into the 'X' mark left by the sword forge deep into the metallic heart of the Draknorr Kilmister and into Draknorr's heart. The living sword let out a piercing scream, its form dissolving into smoke before vanishing completely, taking the spirit of the unwilling slave Kilmister with the dying smoke.

Tin'Old sank to his knees, his strength spent. The sounds of battle faded away, replaced by the gentle rustling of leaves in the breeze. He knew his time was at an end.

"My dear kingdom," Tin'Old said, his voice barely a whisper. "I have fought for you with all that I am. May you prosper long after I leave this world. I welcome Valhalla now."

With those final words, King Tin'Old closed his eyes, his spirit leaving his body and ascending to the heavens. Valkyrja cradled her father's head in her lap as she had done so many years before during his first death. Her tears flowed freely. This time, the pain was greater as she knew the sacrifice the great King had made. The cowardly King was redeemed. Long live the spirit of the brave King Tin'Old.

Artifact Fifteen

The Battle for the Palace Of Stone

orrusta fyrir steinhöllina

ᛟᚱᚢᛖᛏᚠ ᚹᛁᚱᛁᚱ ᛲᛏᛘᛁᛏᚺᛟᚱᛁᛏᚠ

Date: Dimension of Óðinn 140 CE

Underforest Lands

"If there were anyone who had earned the right to call me by my farm maiden name, it would be you, my friend."

Queen Valkyrja stood at the forefront of the army of Arom, her sword gleaming in the sunlight as she surveyed the battlefield. Across from her, the evil Hrothgorn army, a formidable force led by the ruthless General Kors' second in command, Zal'rok, prepared for battle. The air was thick with tension as the two armies faced off, ancient weapons clashing with modern warfare.

"Prepare yourselves, warriors of Arom! You have been freed from the clutches of Draknorr, and now you will fight for the Kingdom of Arom once again!" Queen Valkyrja's voice boomed, rallying her troops. "Today, we fight not just for our land, but for our families, honor, and justice!"

The Hrothgorn army let out a deafening roar in response, their numbers vast and their armor gleaming ominously in the sunlight. Without their King Draknorr, defeated in a fierce battle against King Tin'Old, they were without a true leader, but their thirst for conquest burned as fiercely as ever.

As the two armies charged towards each other, the ground trembled beneath their feet. Arrows rained down from the sky, ancient catapults launched projectiles through the air, and modern tanks rolled into position, their cannons ready to fire. The clash of weapons filled the air with a symphony of battle cries and metal upon metal.

Zal'rok, a towering figure clad in black armor, raised his sword high and bellowed a challenge to Queen Valkyrja. "You may have defeated our king, but you will never defeat the might of the Hrothgorn army! Today, Arom will fall!"

Queen Valkyrja's eyes blazed with determination as she met Zal'rok's gaze. "We may be outnumbered, but we fight with the strength of our convictions and the righteousness of our cause! We will not falter!"

The battle raged on, each side gaining and losing ground in equal measure. Queen Valkyrja, her sword a blur of motion as she struck down enemy after enemy, led her troops with unyielding courage. The Hrothgorn army, their ranks bolstered by dark magic and twisted creatures, fought with a ferocity that seemed almost inhuman.

During the chaos, a flash of light caught Queen Valkyrja's eye. High above the battlefield, a figure clad in shining armor descended from the sky. It was Morning Fire of the Sky with Dragonwülf high atop her scaly spine.

"I was just thinking that what this battle needed was a dragon!" the Queen said. "It was almost as if you had read my thoughts, my dear Dragonwülf."

Dragonwülf and Queen Valkyrja found themselves encircled by the menacing forces of the Hrothgorn army, led by the ruthless warlord Zal'rok. The battlefield was a chaotic scene of clashing swords, grunts of exertion, and the thunderous roars of mythical beasts.

Dragonwülf, with his armor gleaming under the sunlight, stood with the Dragon of Eldora at his side. The dragon's scales shimmered in various shades of blue and green, its eyes ablaze with fierce determination. Queen Valkyrja, a vision of strength and beauty in her golden armor, wielded her enchanted spear with grace and power.

Zal'rok, a towering figure clad in dark armor adorned with menacing spikes, sneered at his opponents. "You stand no chance against the might of the Hrothgorn army!" he bellowed, his voice dripping with malice.

Dragonwülf raised his sword, a blade forged by the ancients in the Iron Mountains, and shouted with a mighty battle cry as he charged forward, the dragon soaring above him, unleashing torrents of flames upon the enemy ranks.

Queen Valkyrja twirled her spear expertly, her movements a dance of lethal precision. "For honor and for glory!" she cried out as she engaged the enemy warriors with unmatched skill and ferocity.

The battlefield became a whirlwind of steel and fire, the clash of weapons and the roar of the dragon echoing across the land. Dragonwülf fought with unparalleled bravery, his sword flashing like lightning, cutting down enemy soldiers with each swing.

Meanwhile, Queen Valkyrja moved with grace and swiftness, her spear striking true against her foes. The Hrothgorn army, taken aback by the sheer determination and prowess of their adversaries, began to falter under the relentless assault.

Zal'rok, seeing his forces weakened, bellowed in rage and launched himself at Dragonwülf with a savage roar. The two warriors clashed in a titanic struggle, their swords meeting in a shower of sparks, each blow shaking the ground beneath them.

The dragon, sensing its master in danger, swooped down with a deafening roar, its jaws dripping with molten fire. With a mighty breath, it unleashed a torrent of flames that engulfed Zal'rok, the evil warlord, screaming in agony as he was consumed by dragon fire. As the last remnants of the Hrothgorn army retreated in disarray, Dragonwülf and Queen Valkyrja stood victorious on the battlefield, their chests heaving with exertion but their spirits high. The Palace of Stone was safe once more, thanks to the bravery and valor of its legendary warriors.

Victory belonged to Queen Valkyrja and the brave warriors of Arom. As they celebrated their hard-won triumph, the echoes of battle faded into the distance, leaving behind only the stories of the brave.

In the aftermath of the epic battle, Queen Valkyrja stood in the clearing, surveying the scorched earth and the remnants of the once-threatening enemy forces. Her heart was heavy with the weight of the losses suffered on both sides. The air was thick with the acrid smell of smoke and blood, a bitter reminder of the violence that had taken place.

As she took a moment to gather her thoughts, a shadow fell over her. Looking up, she saw Morning Fire of the Sky descending from the sky. The dragon's scales gleamed like polished armor in the sunlight, and its eyes held a wisdom that transcended its fearsome appearance.

"Queen Valkyrja," Morning Fire of the Sky rumbled, her voice like distant thunder. "The battle was won, but at great cost. The land may heal, but the wounds of war run deep."

Valkyrja nodded solemnly, her gaze meeting the dragon's luminous eyes. "I know," she replied, her voice tinged with regret. "But we fought for the greater good, to protect our people and our kingdom."

The dragon inclined her head in a silent understanding passing between them. For a moment, the only sounds were the rustling of leaves in the breeze and the distant cries of birds circling overhead.

Finally, Morning Fire of the Sky spoke again, her voice soft yet filled with power. "You have shown great strength and courage, Queen Valkyrja. Your people are fortunate to have you."

Touched by the dragon's words, Valkyrja felt a lump form in her throat. She reached out a hand, tentative yet filled with gratitude, and placed it on the dragon's massive snout." I am grateful for your help in our time of need. Without you, our victory would not have been possible."

The dragon nuzzled her hand gently, a gesture of comfort and solidarity. In that moment, a bond formed between them that transcended the boundaries of species and language.

As she stood there, lost in her thoughts, a deep voice broke through the stillness of the evening air. "My Queen," Dragonwülf said, filled with both reverence and concern.

Valkyrja turned to see Dragonwülf at the cliff's edge, his piercing gaze fixed on the horizon as well. "The cost was great, my Queen," he acknowledged, his voice rough with unspoken emotions. "But the victory was necessary. The people are safe once more because of your bravery and leadership."

Valkyrja nodded, her fingers clenching and unclenching at her sides. "I know, but at what cost?" she repeated, her voice barely above a whisper. "There is so much bloodshed, and so much sacrifice."

Dragonwülf placed a comforting hand on her shoulder, his touch a grounding presence in her turmoil. "There was no other way, my Queen," he said firmly, his eyes locking with hers. "You did what had to be done to protect our lands and our people. You are a warrior, a queen, and a beacon of hope in a world consumed by darkness."

Tears welled up in Valkyrja's eyes as she looked at Dragonwülf, her heart overflowing with gratitude and sorrow. "Thank you, my friend," she whispered, her voice filled with raw emotion. "I could not have done this without you by my side."

Dragonwülf pulled her into a tight embrace, his silent strength a comforting presence in her moment of weakness. "You are not alone, Valorii," he murmured, his voice gentle yet unwavering. "We are in this together, now and always.

"I have not heard that name in many seasons. I like the sound of it, especially coming from you," said the Queen.

"Forgive me, my Queen, I was caught up in the moment, and I did not mean to be so familiar, "said Dragonwülf.

"If there were anyone who had earned the right to call me by my farm maiden name, it would be you, my friend."

The two looked awkwardly into each other's eyes and abruptly turned away as if some unspoken secret had been released into the air.

Forgive me, my Queen, but I must return to the Deepwater at once. We have much work to do," said Dragonwülf. "We have destroyed the enemy of Arom and our Kingdom, but the Defiler still lives, and he must be stopped."

"Return to me safely, my Wolfclaw," said the Queen.

As the last rays of sunlight painted the sky in shades of crimson and gold, Queen Valkyrja and Dragonwülf stood together at the edge of the cliff, their bond unbreakable, their spirits united in a shared purpose that transcended mere words. In that moment of quiet understanding, they found solace in each other's presence, drawing strength from the unspoken connection that bound them together as warriors, as friends, as kindred souls in a world filled with both darkness and light.

Dragonwülf climbed atop Morning Fire and ascended into the dark sky.

Artifact Sixteen

The Death of Snærheimr
dauði Snrheims
ᛗᚨᛚᚾᚦᛁ ᛖᛏᚱᚺᛗᛁᛗᛖ

Date: Dimension of Óðinn 140 CE
Underforest Lands

"Snærheimr may fall, but its spirit will endure."

In the frozen expanse of the galaxy, nestled between twinkling stars and drifting nebulae, lies a planet unlike any other - Snærheimr. This shimmering snow world was a haven of tranquility, where the icy winds carried whispers of ancient tales and the soft snowfall blanketed the land in serene quietness.

Guarding the borders of Snærheimr are the fearsome frost giants, towering figures of immense strength and unwavering loyalty. Despite their intimidating appearance, these guardians are gentle at heart, and they must protect the planet and its inhabitants from any harm that may come their way.

One crisp morning, as the sun peeked over the horizon, casting a rosy glow across the icy landscape, a group of travelers arrived at the gates of Snærheimr. Among them was Avat'or of the Destiny of Tyr. The travelers had followed the path of the great titan, the Götterdämmerung.

As the gates opened, Avat'or and his companions were greeted by the towering frost giants, their frost-kissed armor gleaming in the morning light. The leader of the giants, a wise figure named Thrym, stepped forward, his voice rumbling like distant thunder.

"Greetings, travelers, and welcome to Snærheimr, where peace reigns, and harmony thrives," Thrym proclaimed. The people of our realm are known as the "Frostfolk."

Avat'or was struck by the beauty of Snærheimr, the crystalline structures that sparkled like diamonds in the sunlight, and the gentle hum of the wind as it danced through the icy plains.

In the mystical realm of Snærheimr, where snow-capped mountains reached for the sky, and the aurora danced across the night, a shadow loomed on the horizon. The Defiler, a dark and malevolent being, stirred in the depths of the Netherworld, seeking to unleash chaos and destruction upon the peaceful planet.

The Frostfolk of Snærheimr lived in harmony with nature, their homes shimmering like diamonds in the frosty air. Yet, unbeknownst to them, the destiny of their world was about to be forever altered. It was then that the Destiny of Tyr convened in the heart of the icy tundra to discuss the impending threat with the leaders of the planet.

"Friends, the time has come for us to heed the whispers of the wind and prepare for the storm that approaches," declared Avat'or. "The Defiler has turned his evil eye toward you, and his hunger for power is driving him to this doorstep. The peace-loving people of Snærheimr make them a target for evil."

"Who or what is this Defiler?" asked Thrym. "Why should we fear him?"

"We have pursued him throughout the galaxy, and his ship is barreling toward Snærheimr with much speed," warned Avat'or. The renegade god strikes fear wherever he goes and destroys the balance of good versus evil in the universe."

The gathered council of the winter planet murmured in alarm, their faces etched with worry and fear.

"We must summon Queen Rhiannon at once!" ordered Thrym. Our Queen will save us from this evil! She visits the hill people and the far side of the city. Bring her at once!"

Thrym was known for his bravery and skill with a blade, a skill not usually found in the fierce and brave frost giants. His eyes blazed with determination as he spoke up, "We will give our all to protect our land and our people."

Avat'or raised a weathered hand, his ancient staff glinting in the pale light of the moon. "We must unite and stand together against this dark force," he said. "We cannot face the Defiler alone. We must seek aid from beyond our world, from realms unknown to you."

"Who are these that you seek?" asked the giant.

"We will summon the fellowship of Dragonwülf and the crew of the Deepwater Watchman. They will be here shortly," said Avat'or. "If anyone can do battle with The Defiler, it is one such as Dragonwülf."

As the council deliberated on its next course of action, a sudden gust of wind swept through the chamber, carrying with it a chilling warning.

"Beware, for the Defiler's minions approach," whispered the wind, its voice ghostly and otherworldly. "Their shadow falls across the land, heralding doom and despair."

Just then, a messenger burst into the chamber, his breath ragged and his eyes wide with panic. "Elder Thrym, the enemy is at our gates!" he cried, his words echoing through the chamber like a thunderclap.

The Destiny of Tyr rose as one, their resolve steeling like the blade of a warrior before the battle. "To arms, my brothers! We shall not cower in the face of darkness!" shouted Avat'or, his voice ringing with authority and defiance.

The Frostfolk of Snærheimr rallied together, their hearts filled with courage and hope. As the first rays of dawn broke over the horizon, the fate of their world was uncertain, poised between the light of salvation and the darkness of annihilation. The battle for Snærheimr had begun, and The Defiler would soon know the strength and tenacity of those who called this icy planet their home.

As the Götterdämmerung emerged from the depths of space, casting a shadow over the planet, the inhabitants of Snærheimr knew that their peaceful existence was about to be shattered. The planet killer loomed ominously in the sky, its weapons primed and ready to unleash unimaginable destruction.

The leaders of Snærheimr, including Queen Rhiannon and the Council of Elders, gathered to discuss their strategy in the face of such a relentless enemy. They knew that they had to fight to protect their beloved planet, even if the odds seemed insurmountable.

Queen Rhiannon, a wise and courageous ruler, addressed her people, her voice steady and resolute.

"We may be facing our greatest challenge yet, but we will not cower in the face of this darkness. We will stand together and defend Snærheimr with all that we have."

The planet destroyer descended to the surface of the winter planet, softly resting on four points in the snow.

The Defiler, a towering figure clad in dark armor, descended from a large hatch at the bottom of the Götterdämmerung, its eyes burning with malice and hatred. "Snærheimr will fall before me," he hissed, his voice filled with menace. "If the Destiny of Tyr promises protection… They lie. I have come to claim this planet as my own," his voice echoing like thunder. "Surrender now, or face the consequences."

A great battle loomed as the forces of Snærheimr prepared to clash with the Defiler's minions; the air filled with the sound of the preparation of weapons and war cries. The planet itself seemed to tremble under the weight of the conflict, the very earth crying out in anguish.

A fierce battle was about to unfold. The Queen of Snærheimr, Rhiannon, stood at the forefront of her people, ready to face the impending threat. The ominous killer planet known as the Götterdämmerung loomed in the sky, its dark presence casting a shadow over Snærheimr.

Just as hope seemed to dwindle, a figure emerged from the icy horizon. It descended like a regal bird from the heavens. It was the form of the Deepwater Watchman. Dragonwülf, with a mighty sword in hand and determination in his eyes, approached Queen Rhiannon.

"Queen Rhiannon, fear not, for I am Dragonwülf, and I have come to aid you in this time of need," he declared, his voice unwavering.

Rhiannon looked at Dragonwülf with gratitude and relief. "Thank you, noble warrior. Your presence gives us hope in this dark hour. Together, we shall defend Snærheimr against the evil that threatens us."

"Queen Rhiannon, your time has come. Surrender your planet to me, or face the consequences," the Defiler sneered, his eyes glowing with dark power.

Dragonwülf stepped forward, his sword gleaming in the icy light. "We shall never surrender to one as wicked as you, Defiler. Snærheimr will stand strong against your tyranny."

As the battle ensued, swords clashed, magic crackled in the air, and the fate of Snærheimr was uncertain. The warriors fought with valor and determination, their cries echoing across the frozen landscape.

During the battle, Queen Rhiannon called out to Dragonwülf, her voice filled with urgency. "Dragonwülf, we must unite our strengths and end this darkness. Together, we can overcome any foe."

With a nod of agreement, Dragonwülf and Rhiannon fought side by side, their unity strengthening their resolve. As they faced the Defiler in a final showdown, Dragonwülf's sword clashed with the dark energies of their enemy.

Queen Rhiannon fought bravely at the forefront of the battle, her sword flashing in the sunlight as she faced off against the Defiler itself. "You will not destroy what we have built," she declared, her eyes blazing with determination.

The Defiler laughed a terrifying laugh that sent shivers down the spines of all who heard it. "Your defiance means nothing," it sneered. "Snærheimr will fall, and I will not kill you, so you will witness its end."

The Queen would not be deterred. With a mighty cry, she struck a decisive blow against the Defiler's minion, sending it staggering back. The forces of Snærheimr rallied behind their Queen, fighting with unparalleled courage and resilience.

As the Götterdämmerung unleashed its devastating arsenal upon the planet, the defenders of Snærheimr fought with all their might, refusing to back down in the face of overwhelming odds. The skies blazed with fire and destruction, but still, the people of Snærheimr stood strong.

As the fires blazed, a dark shadow descended upon Snærheimr. The ground trembled, and the sky turned as black as night.

"You pitiful creatures, you refused to bend the knee to me, your true god," The Defiler bellowed, his voice echoing like thunder across the planet. "Your world is now mine to conquer and destroy."

The Frostfolk gathered in fear.

"Why do you seek to harm us?" a frost giant asked, his words laced with sorrow. "We have done you no wrong."

The Defiler sneered, his dark eyes gleaming with malevolent delight. "Your innocence means nothing to me, Frost Giant! I am the bringer of chaos and destruction, and I will bring about the end of Snærheimr."

With a sinister grin, the Defiler raised his hand, and a wave of dark energy surged forth, shattering the ground beneath him. The once pristine landscapes of Snærheimr now lie in ruins, consumed by flames and darkness.

The Frostfolk cried out in despair as their homes and lives were taken before their very eyes. Dragonwülf stood tall, his heart heavy with grief, but his spirit broken.

"Quickly, Majesty, you must gather your elders and come aboard the Deepwater. We can save the essence of your society. It is not too late! Please come with me!" said a pleading Dragonwülf.

The Defiler laughed with a cruel sound that filled the air with dread. "Your hope is meaningless. I am the bringer of annihilation, and nothing can stand in my way."

"No brave Dragonwülf, I must remain among my people and the ones I love."

"This serves no purpose for you to die along with your elders! The Destiny of Tyr will save you!" pleaded Dragonwülf.

"I am already saved. I am with my people. The Frostfolk have already saved me, and I them."

As the people of Snærheimr watched in horror, The Defiler activated The Götterdämmerung's weapons, harnessing its destructive power to unleash a cataclysmic force unlike anything the galaxy had ever seen. The once vibrant planet trembled and shook as the weapon charged, casting a dark shadow over the land.

"Your reign ends here and now, so-called Queen," he proclaimed, his eyes blazing with determination.

As the battle raged on, The Defiler unleashed the full power of The Götterdämmerung, aiming its destructive force at the heart of Snærheimr. The Frostfolk, united in purpose and resolve, stood their ground against the overwhelming power of their foe.

"You cannot destroy that which is eternal," Queen Rhiannon said, her voice filled with desperate assurance. "Snærheimr may fall, but its spirit will endure."

Very well then, if Snærheimr will not bow to me and become mine, it will belong to no one!"

In the final moments before the planet's destruction, the Destiny of Tyr and Dragonwülf were lifted aboard the Deepwater and sailed into the stratosphere.

Queen Rhiannon closed her eyes and whispered a silent prayer to the universe. "May our light never fade," she spoke, as the planet Snærheimr imploded in a brilliant burst of energy that spiraled out into the void, leaving behind nothing but stardust and memories of a once-beautiful world.

As the echoes of Snærheimr faded into the vast expanse of space, a new star was born from the ashes - a symbol of hope and sacrifice that would shine for eternity, a reminder of the courage and love that once thrived on a planet lost to the annals of time.

In the aftermath of the catastrophic destruction of Snærheimr, Dragonwülf and crew traveled through space and time once again.

"What good are these powers of time that we have if they can do no good for innocents like these?" Dragonwülf lamented.

The once vibrant and thriving world now lay in ruins, the remnants of its civilization scattered like ashes in the wind. The sky was filled with smoke, the ground scorched and broken.

Dragonwülf knelt before Avat'or, his hands running over the worn features of the face that once greeted him each morning. "How could this have happened?" he whispered, his voice filled with pain.

A voice from behind him answered, "The darkness came swiftly, swallowing everything in its path."

Dragonwülf turned to see a figure cloaked in shadow standing before him. It was Queen Rhiannon; her eyes were filled with tears as she spoke of the tragedy that had befallen their world.

"Óðinn has allowed me a visit in spirit with you before my journey to Valhalla," she said with an assuring smile." We were not prepared for the power that descended upon us," she continued, her voice trembling with emotion. "The forces of destruction swept through our defenses like a tidal wave, leaving nothing but devastation in their wake."

Dragonwülf clenched his fists in anger, his jaw set with determination. "We cannot let this stand. We must rise from the ashes and fight back against the darkness that threatens to consume us all."

Rhiannon placed a hand on Dragonwülf's shoulder, her touch comforting yet filled with a sense of urgency. "You carry the flame of hope within you, Dragonwülf. Let it guide you in the darkness that surrounds us."

With renewed resolve, Dragonwülf stood tall, his eyes blazing with determination. "I swear on the ashes of Snærheimr that I will not rest until we have avenged your fallen brothers and sisters. The darkness may have taken your world, but it will never extinguish the light that burns within all of us."

"I will avenge your people, brave Queen. Sleep well in your eternal sleep," said Dragonwülf as he touched the Queen's hand one last time. His mind wandered back to his own Queen of Arom, and he wondered where she might be this night.

Artifact Seventeen

Madman Across the Universe

**Date: Dimension of Frigg 1894 CE-
Earth/ Sir Robert Winterfall expedition**

"Remember, my friends, the world is vast and full of wonders. Go forth with courage in your hearts, and you shall find adventure at every turn."

As we pursue The Defiler across the universe, let the chronicles of Dragonwülf and the Destiny of Tyr be written for all time, a testament to the unbreakable bonds that bind us across the ages," proclaimed Sir Robert Winterfall from the deck of the Deepwater Watchman. He was furiously writing a record of all of the occurrences on the ship for those who would find them in the Panorama of Time. It was time for him to reconcile his timeline and make right his universe as promised by the Destiny of Tyr.

"I have been patient, old boy," he said, speaking to Dragonwülf. "I have seen our shipmates sent to their timelines, but there does not seem to be redemption in that book of dreams those Destiny chaps have."

"Have no fear, good Sir," said Dragonwülf. "Your timeline must be preserved at all costs. You and it are very special."

"What does that mean? Are you just trying to appease me?' asked Sir Robert.

"Nay... not at all. Your written record is to be part of a larger one yet to be discovered. It will bring all people together in one civilization and in one mind."

"How can you know this, my old friend?" asked Sir Robert.

"This you will just have to believe, but in the meantime, The Deepwater will carry you back to your time in London to reconcile your history. I hope in the names of our gods that you are redeemed as you wish.

The Written History of Sir Robert Winterfall

In the year 1892, Sir Robert Winterfall, a renowned 19th-century explorer, set out on a daring expedition to the uncharted forests of Norway. Armed with his unwavering curiosity and a deep passion for discovery, Winterfall was determined to uncover the secrets hidden beneath the land and forests in what is now present-day Norway.

As Winterfall ventured deeper into the heart of the Norwegian wilderness, he encountered numerous obstacles and challenges. From treacherous terrain to unpredictable weather, the explorer faced it all with stoic determination and unwavering resolve. Despite the hardships of the journey, Winterfall's spirits remained high, fueled by the insatiable thirst for knowledge that burned within him.

One fateful day, while traversing through a particularly dense part of the forest, Winterfall stumbled upon a hidden entrance concealed beneath a veil of tangled vines and ancient moss under a large tree. Intrigued by the mysterious opening, the explorer wasted no time in stepping inside.

What Winterfall discovered within the depths of the underground caverns was beyond anything he could have ever imagined. A sprawling civilization, untouched by time, lay hidden beneath the surface of the Earth. Magnificent structures carved from stone, intricate hieroglyphs adorning the walls, and a sense of ancient wisdom lingering in the air - all pointed to a civilization lost to the annals of history. He was led through the base of a tall pine tree and through several passages. There he was led to the Palace of Stone.

Captivated by the wonder and awe of his discovery, Winterfall meticulously documented his findings, recording every detail with precision and care.

The explorer's accounts were filled with vivid descriptions of the underground city, its inhabitants, and the customs that governed their way of life.

"We stand on the cusp of a revelation that will reshape our understanding of history and our place in the tapestry of the world." He wrote in his journal.

Winterfall's groundbreaking discoveries soon made waves in the academic and scientific communities, sparking debates and discussions about the existence of lost civilizations and the untapped potential of the natural world. His accounts of the underground civilization beneath the forests of Norway catapulted him to fame, but for all the wrong reasons.

Sir Robert Winterfall stood before a crowd of skeptical scholars as he recounted his incredible discovery. "Gentlemen, I assure you, what I have found beneath the mountains of Norway is beyond anything we could have imagined," he exclaimed, his voice filled with fervor.

The scholars murmured amongst themselves, exchanging skeptical glances. One of them, a distinguished professor with a disdainful expression, spoke up. "Dr. Winterfall, do you truly expect us to believe that you have discovered a passage to an underground civilization? Such fanciful tales have no place in the realm of science." His comments were followed by uncomfortable laughter.

Winterfall's brow furrowed, his determination evident. "I swear to you, gentlemen, it is the truth! I stumbled upon a hidden entrance while conducting geological surveys in the region, and what I found below the surface was astounding. A vast network of tunnels, illuminated by strange glowing crystals, led me to a civilization unlike any known to man."

Another scholar scoffed. "Where is this supposed underground civilization? Why have we not heard of it before if it truly exists?"

Winterfall's eyes gleamed with intensity as he responded, "The passage is well hidden, accessible only to those who know where to look. I implore you to come with me and see for yourselves. Witness the wonders that lie beneath our very feet."

The scholars shook their heads, unconvinced by Winterfall's impassioned plea. As they began to disperse, one by one and two by two, muttering about the explorer's descent into madness, Winterfall's voice rose above the din. "I will not be deterred by your disbelief! I will continue to explore the underground realm, to uncover its secrets and prove to the world that I speak the truth!"

Days turned into weeks, and weeks into months, as Winterfall delved deeper into his notes, arranging his discoveries in meticulous detail. His journals overflowed with intricate maps and sketches of strange architecture, and his descriptions of the underground civilization grew more elaborate with each passing day. He was ready to attempt one more presentation to the British Archeological Society.

One evening, as the scholars gathered once again to hear Sir Winterfall's latest findings, they were met with a sight that sent shivers down their spines. The explorer stood before them, his eyes wild and his voice filled with an otherworldly fervor. His white hair stood on end as if he had seen specters, and his clothing was wrinkled, matted, and dirty. His voice shook with emotion.

"I have seen the wonders of the underground realm, the beauty of its architecture, and the wisdom of its inhabitants," he cried, his words echoing through the room. "I have communed with the dwellers of the deep, learned their ancient ways, and been forever changed by what I have witnessed."

The scholars exchanged uneasy glances, unsure of what to make of his transformation. One brave soul stepped forward, his voice hesitant. "Sir Winterfall, are you feeling quite well? Your words are... troubling, to say the least."

He paid no heed, his gaze fixed on some unseen horizon. "I have been blessed with visions of a world beyond our own, a realm of infinite possibility and unimaginable wonders. I am no longer bound by the constraints of this mortal realm, for I have glimpsed the truth of the underground civilization, and it has set my soul ablaze."

With those cryptic words, Sir Robert Winterfall turned and disappeared into the shadows, leaving the scholars to wonder whether his discovery was indeed a product of a brilliant mind or a descent into madness beyond their comprehension.

Dr. Winterfall was later reported missing by his family. The only thing that was left in his library at the Winterfall estate was his meticulous notes and several piles of wet seaweed on his desk. His body was never located.

The Destiny of Tyr Connection

As the Deepwater approached the corridor of time, Sir Robert found himself in the orderliness of 19th-century Victorian-era London, England. Dragonwülf and The Destiny were very careful to return the good Doctor to a point sometime before his death and resurrection. Still, an archeologist who was ridiculed and disgraced, he sought and found solace in the company of a few loyal friends, including Miss Lillian Abernathy, a brilliant mathematician who understood the mysteries that plagued his mind.

On that brisk autumn evening, as the fog enveloped the gas-lit streets of London, Dr. Winterfall sat by the fireplace in his dimly lit study, surrounded by dusty books and artifacts from distant lands. Miss Abernathy, her curly hair pinned back, her analytical gaze fixed on him, broke the silence that hung heavy in the room.

"Robert, you cannot continue down this path of obscurity. Society will never accept your theories unless you provide concrete evidence," she said, her voice firm yet laced with concern.

Dr. Winterfall turned to her, his eyes gleaming with a spark of defiance. "Lillian, you of all people should understand that the truth is not always tangible. Sometimes it lies in the spaces between what we see and what we believe."

They lapsed into contemplative silence until a knock at the door interrupted their discourse. A young messenger stood at the threshold, holding a letter addressed to Dr. Winterfall. With trembling hands, he broke the seal and read its contents, his expression shifting from curiosity to astonishment.

"It's from an anonymous benefactor, pledging support for my next expedition," he murmured, barely able to contain his excitement.

Miss Abernathy leaned forward, her eyes scanning the letter. "This is a remarkable opportunity, Robert," she said. "Perhaps this may help in your cause to vindicate yourself.

Determined and fueled by newfound hope, Dr. Winterfall embarked on his most ambitious journey yet - a quest to uncover the lost city of DragonBorne, a mythical civilization rumored to have transcended time itself.

With a team of seasoned explorers and scholars at his side, he traversed treacherous jungles and crossed vast deserts, following ancient maps and enigmatic clues that led them ever closer to their elusive destination.

As they approached the rumored location of the lost city of Arom, a sense of awe and foreboding gripped the expedition. The air crackled with energy, the very atmosphere seemingly alive with whispers of forgotten ages. There, amidst the ruins of a once-great city, Winterfall beheld a sight that would reshape history itself.

In a hidden chamber deep beneath the earth, he discovered a device unlike any known to man - a device that shimmered with otherworldly energy, pulsing with the heartbeat of a civilization long lost to time. As he reached out to touch it, a blinding light enveloped him, and the world around him dissolved into a kaleidoscope of colors and shapes.

The Discovery of the Hourglass

Robert's hands trembled with excitement as he held in his hands the mysterious obsidian hourglass. His heart raced as he repeated the ancient phrase printed in white letters aloud, "Saela linoo eir, *reveal your shards of time.* "The chamber grew quiet, the only sound being the echo of his voice against the walls.

Suddenly, a low hum filled the air, and a warm glow emanated from the hourglass's core. It was as if the room itself had come to life. Colors swirled within the glass, dancing as if spirits were trapped within its confines.

Sir Robert hesitated for a moment before finally summoning the courage to touch the center of the hourglass. As his fingertips made contact, a surge of energy pulsed through him, sending shivers down his spine. The room around him began to fade away, replaced by a blinding light.

When the light finally subsided, Robert found himself standing in a vast chamber surrounded by towering pillars adorned with glowing symbols. He realized that he had been transported not just through space but also through time itself.

A voice, ancient and wise, filled the chamber. "Welcome, seeker of knowledge. You have unlocked the secrets of the hourglass, a bridge between the past and the future. What is it that you seek?"

Robert's mind raced with questions, but one burned brighter than the rest. "I seek to understand the mysteries of time, to unlock its secrets and uncover the truths hidden within its depths."

The voice chuckled softly. "A noble quest, indeed. Time is a river, ever flowing and ever changing. To understand its nature, one must first understand oneself. Look within, seeker, and you shall find the answers you seek."

With those words, the chamber began to fade, and Robert felt himself being pulled back through the vortex of time. As he opened his eyes, he found himself once again in his study, the *obsidian hourglass* glowing softly before him.

Later, he presented his conclusive findings to 'The Grand Society of Archeology. Dressed in an attire of faded but respectable tweed, Winterfall's hands trembled only slightly as he clutched his hourglass. His once piercing blue eyes, now glazed with age and hardship, used his cane as more than a fashionable accouterment. He looked at the grand hall filled with esteemed colleagues, their skeptical eyes scrutinizing his every move. In his heart vibrated a battle cry, a desperate plea for redemption.

With a voice steadier than his beating heart, Winterfall began to present. He weaved narratives of ancient civilizations, each interconnected by the thread of time travelers. His passages were denser than the deepest forests, his arguments as compelling. From the Mayans' intricate calendar and the construction of the great Pyramids to the cryptic texts of the Dead Sea Scrolls and the enigma of Stonehenge, Winterfall convincingly relates all these events to the curious case of time voyagers.

Ingenious diagrams of time-traveling devices, sketches of outlandish garments worn by these chronological adventurers, and pages of deciphered codes were presented stunningly. His years of tireless effort materialized before the assembly seemed to lend proof that Winterfall was indeed a lunatic chasing fantasy rather than a scholar pursuing truth.

As he ended his presentation with a fervent plea, "See not with eyes of doubt but with minds open to possibilities," the hall greeted it with a seemingly unending silence.

Sir Robert stood in front of his colleagues holding the hourglass up in his hands at arm's length. The hourglass was unlike any other, with a soft, mystical glow emanating from within.

"What in heaven's name do you have, Winterfall?" asked one of his colleagues, a young geologist named Emily Brownstone. "How much longer are we to be held ransom to your flights of ridiculous fantasy? Enough, I say!"

"I have studied the ancient texts thoroughly," replied Sir Winterfall confidently. "I have a time-traveling hourglass, and it is the key to unlocking the secrets of the lost civilization that lies beneath the forests of Norway."

The room erupted with smatterings of uncomfortable laughter and gasps as the audience headed toward the exit door. They were frozen in their tracks by what happened next.

With a deep breath, Winterfall turned the hourglass upside down, causing the sand within to swirl and shimmer like liquid gold. A brilliant light enveloped the group, and in an instant, they found themselves standing in a dense forest unlike anything they had ever seen.

As they gazed around in wonder, Sir Winterfall pointed toward a hidden entrance partially concealed by overgrown foliage. "This way, my friends. The entrance to the ancient civilization should be just beyond."

The group followed Winterfall deeper into the forest, the air thick with anticipation and excitement. Suddenly, they stumbled upon a massive stone door, covered in intricate carvings and symbols.

"This must be it," exclaimed Emily, her eyes wide with amazement.

"We are sorry for doubting you, Sir," said Dr. Smithey, who had been one of his worst detractors. "There is no way we could have known this."

Winterfall wasted no time and began deciphering the ancient language inscribed on the door. As he spoke the words aloud, the stone door rumbled and slowly began to open, revealing a vast underground chamber bathed in a soft light.

They stepped inside, their footsteps echoing off the walls as they explored the wonders of the lost civilization. Magnificent sculptures lined the walls, depicting scenes of a bygone era filled with magic and mystique.

"This is incredible," whispered one of the colleagues, awestruck by the beauty that surrounded them.

As they delved deeper into the chamber, they stumbled upon an elderly man sitting cross-legged in meditation. He was dressed in armor and fur, much like a Viking warrior. His eyes snapped open as he sensed their presence, and he greeted them with a wise smile.

"Welcome, travelers," he said in a voice that seemed to carry the weight of centuries. "You have unlocked the secrets of the past and found your way to our hidden realm."

Winterfall stepped forward, his heart racing with excitement. "My colleagues, I would like you to meet a dear friend of mine. This fine gentleman is Wolfclaw Thur'Gold, otherwise known as Dragonwülf."

"Tell us, wise one, what is the purpose of this civilization? Why have we been brought here?" asked Emily.

Dragonwülf's eyes twinkled with ancient knowledge as he spoke. "You have been chosen to witness the magic and wonder of a forgotten time, to learn from our mistakes, and to carry forth the wisdom of the ancients into the future. Sir Robert is or has been one of my crew and has taken part in more than one heroic adventure."

"How can this be? How can we be here in this place at this time?" asked Emily.

"You would do well to listen to what this wise man has to teach all of you. It may change your lives and also change the world," said Dragonwülf.

With newfound understanding, Winterfall and his colleagues spent days exploring the lost civilization, eager to uncover its mysteries and treasures. As they prepared to leave, Dragonwülf bestowed upon them a gift - a small hourglass similar to the one Sir Winterfall had used to travel through time.

"May this hourglass be a reminder of your journey and a guide in your future explorations," Dragonwülf said, his gaze resting upon Winterfall.

With a final farewell, the group stepped through a shimmering portal, returning to their own time with hearts full of wonder and minds teeming with newfound knowledge. The members returned to their meeting hall where they had just left, and one by one, the members of 'The Grand Society of Archeology,' seasoned with years of skepticism, acknowledged the truth that lay before them and stood up in applause. The echo of their clapping hands, a melody restoring Winterfall's dignity and reputation, reverberated throughout the hall.

With their approval, Winterfall's weary eyes filled with vindication and triumph, his life, once tethered to mockery, became a manifestation of courage and undeterred conviction. He held onto his belief, flaunting the existence of time travelers not as a conjecture of an unstable mind but as an undeniable reality.

Dr. Robert Winterfall then became more than a brilliant archaeologist. He rose as an emblem of unyielding determination and a beacon urging explorers to quest beyond the boundaries of perceived reality, forever remembered as an explorer outside the antrum of time. He was now free upon his death to return to the fellowship of Dragonwülf and The Destiny of Tyr.

Artifact Eighteen

Saga Drakúlfs

The Saga of Dragonwülf

ᛊᚠᚷᚠ ᛗᚱᛖᚲᚠᚢᛚᚣᛊ

Date: Dimension of Óðinn 140 CE

Underforest Lands

"Ef þú berst hlið við vini þína,

þótt þú fallir, máttu eigi vera sigraðr."

-Drakúlfr

"If you fight alongside your friends, even if you die, you cannot be vanquished."- Dragonwülf.

The crewmembers of the Deepwater were very much in need of some repose, so they stopped by a fire-lit tavern near the old city of DragonBorne. It had been destroyed two centuries before by the ruthless and bloodthirsty

Hrothgorn. The residents there now were mostly pirates and highwaymen, mostly of a transient nature. The travelers on this day were pirates traveling through the sea of Morak. Dragonwülf and his crew were seated around a roaring, crackling fire, regaling one another with tall tales. What the pirates do not know is that Dragonwülf's stories were exactly as he described them.

"There was a time when I stood alone against the dreaded Ice Serpent of Jotunheim," Dragonwülf remembered. "The creature's icy breath could freeze the bravest warrior in their tracks, but I was not so easily bested. With a roar that shook the very mountains, I plunged my sword into the beast's heart, watching as it crumbled to dust at my feet."

A traveler gasped his eyes wide with disbelief. Never before had he heard such tales of heroism and bravery, of a man who seemed more like a god than a mere mortal. Surely, he was in jest.

"And what of the time you faced the trolls of the Black Marsh?" the traveler asked, eager for more and hoping for more hyperbole.

Dragonwülf smiled with a fierce glint in his eye. "Ah, the Trolls," he mused. "Cunning adversaries, to be sure, but with the help of my loyal companions, we stormed their lair and banished them from our lands forever."

The pirates around him listened in awe, their eyes wide with admiration.

"I have faced foes more fierce than the wildest storm," Dragonwülf continued, his eyes glinting with fierce pride. "I have battled creatures that would make even the bravest warrior quail in fear. But through it all, I have emerged victorious in spirit if not by might."

"One young pirate asked, "What do you mean? Either you were a winner, or you were defeated. Which one was it?"

"I was always victorious! There are times when the circumstances showed us to be defeated, but we fought with honor and for the right reason. This is impossible to defeat. If you fight alongside your friends, even if you die, you cannot be vanquished," said Dragonwülf emphatically.

"I still do not understand," said the young pirate.

"Think of this. When an enemy defeats us, we learn just enough about him to defeat him later. If he kills us in battle, our comrades learn enough about him to defeat him later. We win no matter the outcome."

One young warrior, eager to prove himself, spoke up. "Dragonwülf," he said, his voice trembling with nervous energy, "tell us of your greatest triumph, the battle that defines you as the warrior you are."

Dragonwülf's eyes narrowed as he recalled the battle in question. "Ah, young one," he said, his voice low and dangerous, "that was a battle that would have daunted even the mightiest of warriors. I faced a dragon, a creature of fire and shadow, with scales as hard as iron and teeth as sharp as swords."

The pirates gasped in awe, leaning forward eagerly to hear more.

"I stood before the beast, my sword raised high, and I roared a challenge that shook the very mountains themselves," Dragonwülf continued, his voice rising in intensity. "The dragon breathed a stream of fire at me, but I dodged and weaved, moving with the speed and grace of a hunting wolf. And then, with a single stroke, I plunged my sword into the dragon's heart, and it fell at my feet, vanquished."

The warriors erupted into cheers and applause, their voices ringing through the hall like thunder, raising their horns of mead in a toast to a mighty hero.

Dragonwülf held up a hand for silence, his expression grave.

"My friends," he said in a solemn tone, "remember always that it is not just strength or skill that makes a warrior great. It is courage, honor, and loyalty to one's friends and kin. These are the qualities that define a true warrior."

"I will tell a tale of the great warrior from my own chronicles," said Dragonwülf, one of the heroes of Warshield and the fellowship of Wolfclaw, Olaf of Gandor. Listen to the story, as I know it. In the heart of the mystical Enchanted Forest, where ancient trees whispered secrets of old and the air was heavy with magic, a fierce battle unfolded between Olaf, a legendary warrior with the blood of dragons coursing through his veins, and Ghidorwrath, the monstrous sea serpent who ruled the depths of the ocean.

The clash of titans sent tremors through the very land itself, as Olaf stood tall, his gleaming silver armor reflecting the sunlight filtering through the canopy above. He raised his sword, a weapon forged from the scales of the dragons of yore, its fiery edge humming with untapped power.

Ghidorwrath reared his massive serpentine form, his scales shimmering like a liquid emerald in the dim light. His eyes, dark and deep as the abyss, fixated on Olaf with a primal hunger that sent shivers down the spines of even the bravest creatures of the forest.

Olaf's voice was steady, tinged with a hint of defiance that defied the fear swirling in his heart. 'I fear no creature, no matter how ancient or powerful. Your reign of terror ends today, foul Serpent.'

With a deafening roar that shook the very leaves from the trees, Dragonwülf charged forward, his sword slashing through the air with deadly precision. Olaf countered with a massive tail swipe that sent him crashing into the earth, the impact shattering the ground beneath him.

As the warrior staggered to his feet, bloodied but unbowed, he locked eyes with Ghidorwrath once more. 'You may be a creature of the sea, but I am a warrior born of fire and steel. I will not falter in the face of your wrath.'

Ghidorwrath hissed, his jaws gaping wide to reveal rows of razor-sharp teeth that glinted in the fading sunlight. 'You may have fire in your veins, warrior, but it will not save you from the depths of my domain.'

The battle raged on, a symphony of clashing steel, roaring flames, and thunderous waves that reverberated through the forest. Olaf fought with the strength of a hundred warriors, his resolve unshaken even as fatigue gnawed at his limbs. Ghidorwrath, relentless and cunning, sought to overwhelm him with his sheer size and ferocity.

In a final, desperate gambit, Olaf lunged forward, his sword blazing with the heat of a thousand suns. With a mighty swing, he struck true, driving the blade deep into Ghidorwrath's massive heart.

As the sea serpent's lifeless form crumpled to the forest floor, Dragonwülf stood victorious, his chest heaving with exertion and triumph. The ancient warrior had prevailed against the might of the deep, his courage and skill proving unmatched in the face of even the deadliest of foes.

Among the fallen leaves and the rustling of the trees, Olaf raised his sword to the sky, a silent tribute to the power of will and the indomitable spirit of the warrior's heart.

Dragonwülf knew the tale had inspired the men… and he knew the story was not true as well. He meant to give glory to the deserving, meek, and yet brave member of the fellowship of Wolfclaw, Olaf Son of Gandor. What Olaf lacked in skills in battle, he made up for in bravery.

After Dragonwülf had completed his tale, he rose to his feet and spoke to the crowd.

"I have faced adversaries both on the battlefield and within myself, each obstacle a test of my resolve and determination. Through every victory and defeat, I have learned that true honor is not bestowed, but earned through unwavering commitment and unwavering dedication. Glory is not found in the spoils of war but in the courage to face adversity head-on and emerge triumphant."

"Ay!" The men celebrated in unison.

"I grow old and weary in battle, and I see the winter of my life approaching. As the sun sets on my life, I can look back with pride at the battles fought, the victories won, and the honor upheld. For I have lived a life dedicated to the pursuit of honor, glory, and victory, and in that pursuit, I have found the true meaning of life itself," said Dragonwülf.

In the dimly lit hall, the ancient warrior sat before a crackling fire. His weathered face bore the scars of countless battles, and his eyes held the wisdom of ages long past.

"I have seen the rise and fall of empires, the clash of gods and mortals," Dragonwülf began, his voice deep and resonant." The greatest battle lies before me now."

His companions, young warriors eager for glory, leaned in closer, hanging on his every word. He knew that this would be his last battle, the one that would determine the fate of the realms.

"The Defiler seeks to plunge our world into eternal darkness," Dragonwülf continued, his gaze steely. "He has gathered an army of demons and dark sorcerers, ready to unleash terror upon the land."

"What do we know of this rogue spirit?" asked one of the young warriors. "He cannot be invincible. Certainly, he can be defeated."

"We only know of one experience with mortals, and it was quite by accident," explained Dragonwülf. In the shadowed forests of the Forbidden Realm, a being of immense power roamed freely, feared by all who dared to speak its name. The Defiler was a remarkable sight. Standing ten feet tall, his skin was as dark as the night sky, adorned with glowing runes that seemed to shift and writhe under its touch. His eyes burned with a malevolent light, piercing through the darkness with an otherworldly gaze that struck fear into the hearts of even the bravest warriors.

One fateful night, a brave group of adventurers stumbled upon the lair of The Defiler, driven by tales of treasure and the promise of glory. As they cautiously made their way through the twisted trees and eerie mists that surrounded the god's domain, they could feel its baleful presence growing stronger with each step.

The air grew thick with an evil stench, and the ground beneath their feet trembled as the Defiler emerged from the shadows, its massive form towering over them like a dark colossus. With a voice that seemed to echo from the depths of the underworld, it spoke in a chilling tone, "Who dares to disturb my slumber? You, mortals, shall pay dearly for your folly."

The adventurers, though shaken by the god's ominous presence, stood their ground, readying their weapons for the battle that was about to unfold. The Defiler chuckled darkly, its voice sending shivers down their spines as it taunted them with cryptic riddles and ancient prophecies.

As the clash of steel and magic filled the air, the Defiler unleashed its full power, casting spells of darkness and despair that seemed to consume the very essence of their souls. The adventurers fought with all their might, their hearts filled with courage and determination as they struggled against the overwhelming might of the escaped God.

The Defiler treated the treasure hunters like playthings.

With a final cry of defiance, the adventurers launched their ultimate assault, their weapons blazing with righteous fury as they tried to strike down the escaped God for the last time. The Defiler let out a deafening roar and slammed the bodies of the adventurers against the cliff wall, sending them into frenzies of quivering death," explained an emotional Dragonwülf.

"Where is this scoundrel, and why has he not been stopped?" asked a young warrior.

"The Destiny of Tyr and our crew of the Deepwater Watchman have altered the timelines of history, but have not been able to reconcile the Defiler's imbalance of the universe," explained Dragonwülf. "He weakens, and *we will have him*."

The Search for the Defiler

"The Götterdämmerung approaches, Captain! We must be ready," Dragonwülf said.

Old-Turas nodded grimly, adjusting the course of his ship to intercept the enemy vessel. The Götterdämmerung was a formidable opponent, its dark hull bristling with lethal weaponry.

"We must get close enough to board their ship," Turas said, his jaw clenched with determination.

As the two ships closed in on each other, the tension aboard The Deepwater Watchman was palpable. Sailors moved swiftly about the deck, preparing for the imminent clash with the enemy.

With a thunderous roar, the Deepwater Watchman rammed into the Götterdämmerung at full speed, the impact sending splinters of wood flying in all directions. The sound of creaking timbers and shattering metal filled the air as the two vessels grappled with each other, locked in a deadly embrace.

"We must board their ship!" Dragonwülf shouted, drawing his sword and leaping across the yawning chasm that separated the two vessels. Turas followed close behind, his massive form a whirlwind of destruction as he cut down any enemy that dared stand in their way.

As they fought their way through the twisted corridors of the enemy ship, the Defiler emerged from the shadows, his malevolent presence filling the air with icy dread.

"You fools want to battle the inmates of Caligulis?" the Defiler sneered, his voice drenched in sarcasm. "You must have a death wish."

"We will never succumb to the likes of you, demons!" Turas retorted, his sword gleaming in the dim light.

The vast darkness of space was shattered by the fiery clash between the Deepwater Watchman and the dreaded Götterdämmerung.

The battle commenced with a thunderous explosion as the two ships clashed in a fierce exchange of laser fire. Dragonwülf's crew fought bravely, their shouts and commands filling the air as they battled the evil forces of the Defiler.

As the battle raged on, Dragonwülf and his loyal companions made their way through the winding corridors of the Götterdämmerung, facing off against the Defiler's lost souls set free from Caligulis Q3. With swords clashing and blasters blazing, they fought with unmatched valor, each strike bringing them one step closer to the heart of darkness.

Finally, they reached the heart of the ship, where The Defiler awaited them, a twisted grin on his face. "You may have defeated my lost souls, but you will never defeat me, Dragonwülf," he hissed.

Dragonwülf was undaunted. With a fierce battle cry, he lunged forward, his sword meeting the Defiler in a shower of sparks. The two foes clashed in a whirlwind of steel and fire, their strength matched only by their determination.

In the end, Dragonwülf emerged victorious, his blade held tightly to the heart of the Defiler. They then cast him into chains and held him at sword point on five sides. The evil that had plagued the galaxy for so long was finally subdued thanks to the courage and sacrifice of Dragonwülf and his crew.

In the vast expanse of the heavenly realms, Dragonwülf and the crew of the Deepwater Watchman sailed to deliver their prisoner, the infamous Defiler of Souls, to the council of the old gods for trial.

As the ship cut through the dark waters, the tension on board was palpable. The Defiler, a fearsome sorcerer with eyes like smoldering coals, was shackled and guarded at all times. His mere presence sent shivers down the spines of even the most hardened sailors.

Old- Turas, the stoic captain with a heart as fierce as the stormy seas, stood at the helm, his hands steady despite the roiling waves. His eyes were fixed on the horizon, his mind consumed with thoughts of yet to come.

As the Deepwater Watchman approached the ancient isle where the council of the old gods held court, a feeling of unease settled over the crew. The air was thick with a sense of foreboding as if the very elements themselves were poised to pass judgment.

Upon reaching the shore, Dragonwülf and his crew were greeted by a group of wraithlike beings, their forms shimmering like starlight. These were the envoys of the old gods, sent to escort the Defiler to his trial.

"We have come to deliver the prisoner, as commanded," Dragonwülf said, his voice steady despite the weight of their task.

One of the envoys nodded solemnly. "The council waits. Follow us."

As they made their way through the ancient ruins that housed the council chamber, the Defiler spoke for the first time since his capture. His voice was like a low rumble of thunder, filled with malice and defiance.

"You think your gods can judge me? I am beyond their petty laws," he sneered.

Dragonwülf's jaw clenched, but he remained silent, knowing that words alone would not sway the outcome of the trial.

Finally, they entered the chamber of the old gods, a vast hall filled with swirling mists and flickering torches. The council sat upon thrones of pure gold, their faces obscured by shadows.

The lead envoy stepped forward, his voice resonating with power. "Defiler of Souls, you stand accused of blasphemy and treason against the old gods. How do you plead?"

The Defiler laughed such that it chilled the blood of all who stood in witness. "I plead guilty to nothing. Your gods are weak and blind, unworthy of my allegiance."

The council whispered amongst themselves, their voices like the rustling of leaves in a haunted forest. Finally, the lead envoy spoke again.

"Dragonwülf, captain of the Deepwater Watchman, you have brought this prisoner before us. What do you say in his defense?"

Dragonwülf stepped forward, his gaze unwavering. "I have no defense to offer for his crimes. If it were so up to me, I would kill him with my sword and deliver him unto you as a headless corpse, but I stand by the laws of the old gods, and I trust in their judgment."

"You have no power to do anything like that, you weakling! I am a god! You will feel my wrath before you die!" screamed the Defiler.

"Tonight you shall sleep in Hades, and tonight I will sleep in my quarters. Wrath indeed!" mocked Dragonwülf.

Artifact Nineteen

The Rage of the Old Gods

reiði gamla goðanna

ᚱᛖᛁᚦᛁ ᚷᚨᛗᛚᚨ ᚷᛟᚦᚨᚾᚨ

Date: Future Dimension of Höðr 2296 CE

"Darkness may consume my soul, but it is the world that shall drown in its depths, for when the night falls, and the shadows whisper my name, revenge shall be the melody that guides my hands to paint the world in hues of vengeance."

As the council of the old gods murmured in the grand hall of Asgard, tension crackled in the air like lightning before a storm. The esteemed members - Loki, Frigg, Heimdallr, Thor, and Höðr - sat in a semicircle, their expressions a mixture of grim determination and cautious curiosity. At the center of the room, chained and shackled, was The Defiler.

Óðinn, the All-father, watching from the heavens from his royal throne, fixed his one-eyed gaze upon The Defiler.

"You stand accused of treachery against your fellow gods and of jeopardizing the very fabric of the cosmos. How do you plead?" asked Thor on behalf of his father.

The Defiler, a figure cloaked in shadows and malice, raised his head slowly, his eyes gleaming with a dark light.

"Again, weaklings, I plead guilty to nothing. I have merely done what I must to survive in this world of deceit and betrayal."

Loki, the master of mischief, leaned forward with a smirk playing on his lips." How intriguing. Tell us, Defiler, what drove you to such drastic measures? Surely, there must be a reason for your descent into darkness."

The Defiler chuckled softly, a sound that sent shivers down the spines of those present. "Reason, you say? I have seen the true nature of this world, the hypocrisy of these so-called gods. I sought power to break free from your suffocating grasp, to forge my own destiny."

Frigg, the queen of Asgard, regarded The Defiler with a mix of pity and scorn. "You speak of power, yet all you have brought is ruin and despair. Your actions cannot be justified, no matter the grievances you hold."

Heimdallr, the ever-watchful guardian, raised a hand to silence the murmurs that began to spread among the council. "Enough talk of grievances and justifications. The time has come for judgment upon The Defiler. Speak now, for your fate hangs in the balance."

The Defiler's eyes blazed with defiance as he addressed the council once more. "Do what you must, old gods. Your judgment holds no sway over me. I am beyond your reach, beyond your understanding. In a world consumed by darkness, where shadows dance with malevolence and whispers of revenge echo in the wind, I stand as the harbinger of chaos and despair. Through the corridors of time, I have witnessed the depths of depravity that mortals are capable of, their hearts corrupted by greed and their spirits consumed by hatred. In their folly, they have awoken a beast within me, a beast that thirsts for retribution and craves the taste of their suffering. When the flames of retribution consume this world, they will know that it was I who brought about their downfall."

Heimdallr nodded solemnly, his voice echoing like thunder through the hall. "Then let it be known that The Defiler shall be cast out from the realm of the gods, banished to wander the void for eternity. May his name be forgotten, his deeds a cautionary tale for all who would follow in his dark footsteps."

"You stand accused of heinous crimes against your fellow gods and mortals," Thor boomed, his voice resonating throughout the hall. "How do you plead, Defiler?"

The Defiler sneered defiantly. "I plead guilty to nothing. I have merely sought to carve my own path in this world of gods and men."

Heimdallr raised an eyebrow. "By spreading chaos and destruction in your wake, your actions have endangered the very fabric of the realms."

The Defiler chuckled darkly. "Order and chaos are but two sides of the same coin. I have simply embraced the inevitable."

Frigg shook her head sadly. "Your arrogance knows no bounds. You have brought pain and suffering to countless lives."

Thor stepped forward, his eyes flashing with anger. "You will pay for your crimes, Defiler. You have crossed the line too many times."

The council deliberated, exchanging whispers and glances

"We hereby sentence you to suffer death at the pleasure of Óðinn!" ordered Thor.

The Defiler's eyes widened in shock. "No...You cannot do this! I am a god!"

The Defiler was led away to face his fate, his protests being ignored. As the echoes of his screams faded into the distance, the old gods remained silent, knowing that justice had been served.

In the end, the Defiler was placed in chains to face Óðinn. His screams and his evil laughter rang out like a curse upon the winds.

⸻⸻◇⸻⸻

The Justice of Óðinn

In a sudden and furious clap of thunder and display of lightning, Óðinn appeared from the heavens. He came to rest lightly in the middle of the semicircle of the old gods and the new.

"You have done well in your search for the Defiler. The Destiny of Tyr has done many great things to help balance the universe once again. Our work is not done. I appeared before this council to discuss the execution that shall befall The Defiler," Óðinn thundered. "His crimes are unforgivable, and his very existence threatens the balance of the cosmos."

Frigg, queen of Asgard, raised an eyebrow. "What do you propose, Father Óðinn?"

Óðinn surveyed the room, his gaze settling on Athena, the goddess of wisdom and war. "Athena, you have always been wise beyond your years. What do you say?"

Athena rose gracefully from her throne, her piercing grey eyes fixed on The Defiler. "I have consulted the fates, and they have decreed that The Defiler's soul must be shattered into a thousand fragments and scattered to the winds. Only then can his dark essence be vanquished from this world."

The other gods murmured their agreement, and Óðinn nodded solemnly. "So be it. The Defiler, you have been found guilty of heinous crimes against both mortals and gods. Your sentence is to be carried out immediately."

The Defiler, a towering figure clad in black armor and wreathed in shadows, laughed cruelly. "I am a god as well as you are gods. I am eternal, unstoppable! What punishment can you inflict on another god?"

With a wave of his hand, Óðinn summoned chains of divine energy that bound The Defiler in place. The other gods joined in, their combined power creating a barrier of pure light that surrounded their dark adversary.

Hades, god of the underworld, stepped forward, his voice cold and merciless. "Prepare yourself, Defiler. Your torment begins now."

As the council chanted ancient incantations, the ground rumbled and cracked open, revealing a swirling vortex of darkness beneath The Defiler's feet. With a final roar of defiance, the malevolent monster shattered like shards of glass. The last remnants of the Defiler were dragged down into the abyss, his screams fading into the void.

The gods watched in silence as the earth closed over the portal to the underworld, sealing The Defiler's fate for all eternity. Athena turned to her companions, a fierce light in her eyes.

"The threat has been vanquished," she declared. "Let this serve as a warning to any who would seek to challenge the divine order. We are the gods of old and gods of the new, and we will not hesitate to protect our realm from darkness."

Dragonwülf's work was done for now. The Defiler had been defeated at last. Now he would return to Arom to serve his Queen in 126- 128 BCE.

The Death of a Farm Girl

The night air over the palace of Stone was thick with the scent of molten steel and distant storm. Queen Valkyrja stood at the highest balcony, the banners of her reign fluttering like shadows against the moonlight. The halls below were silent, too silent, as though the castle itself had been holding its breath.

She did not see them come at first. The masked figures slipping through the eastern gate, their armor black as midnight, eyes burning with the unyielding loyalty of a kingdom wronged. The Kingdom of Hrothgorn had come for revenge. King Draknorr's death had left them hollow, hungry for blood. Valkyrja, the mighty Queen of Arom, now must pay.

A dagger sang through the air, a silver flash that caught even the moon off guard. Valkyrja twisted, instinct honed from decades of battle, but the strike was too swift. A second dagger, then a third, and pain exploded across her chest. She staggered, grasping the balcony railing, her breath shallow and ragged. Her crown, heavy with jewels and the weight of duty, slipped forward.

As darkness crept in, Valkyrja's mind fractured, and the visions began.

She was no longer the Queen of Arom. She was Valorii, a young farm girl with calloused hands and dreams bigger than the wheat fields she had once tended. She knelt before the great King Tin'Old, offering the humble fruits of her labor. His eyes were sharp but kind, his voice like thunder softened by warmth.

"Valorii," she remembered him saying, *"Even the smallest hands may shape the destiny of kings."*

She saw herself running through the meadows, chasing the wind, the laughter of a simpler life echoing in her ears. She remembered the nights by the hearth, listening to stories of heroes and gods, daring to dream that she might one day stand among them.

Pain returned, sharper now, burning through her veins. Her body slumped against the cold stone, and the Hrothgorn assassins closed in, their whispers like knives. She tried to speak, to summon the strength to fight, but her voice was lost, swallowed by the night.

Yet, in that final moment, another vision came, but it was not of war, nor of blood, but of triumph and hope. She saw Dragonwülf, ancient and unyielding, standing atop a mountain of stars, Morning Fire of the Sky coiled behind him, eyes blazing like the sun. She saw the Destiny of Tyr, watching, waiting, guiding. She saw the lives she had touched, the legacies she had forged, and the courage she had sparked.

A single tear slipped from her eye, trailing down her cheek like molten silver.

"Do not mourn me," she whispered, though the sound was lost to the wind. *"Remember the girl I once was, and the queen I became. Fight, endure… and rise."*

Then, the darkness swallowed her entirely. The balcony was empty save for the queen's crown, teetering on the edge, catching the first glimmer of dawn as if to mark the passing of an era.

In the distance, the cowardly Hrothgorn assassins retreated, leaving nothing but silence and the faint, lingering echo of a life that had touched the very fabric of the world. Arom mourned, but the seeds of hope she had planted were already taking root—unseen, unbroken, eternal.

Shadows over Arom

The first rays of dawn struck the palace of Stone like shards of silver, illuminating the bloodied balcony where Queen Valkyrja had fallen. The city below was oblivious, unaware that its ruler had been struck down in cold vengeance. Yet the air itself seemed heavier, as though the walls of the castle mourned her passing.

Inside the Great Hall, Dragonwülf felt it first not with his eyes, but with the sudden, undeniable tremor that ran through the weave of the world. The Destiny of Tyr, the unseen force that had guided kingdoms and shaped fates, shivered. A shadow had entered the balance.

"My Queen… is…" whispered Avat'or, his voice cracking as he stumbled over the threshold.

The hall was empty, save for the lingering echoes of Valkyrja's command, her presence now reduced to silence. Blood smeared the stone beneath the balcony, a cruel testament to her final moments.

Dragonwülf, standing silent and immovable as ever, placed a gauntleted hand on the hilt of his sword. Morning Fire of the Sky coiled protectively behind him, smoke curling from her nostrils in a low hiss. Even the dragon sensed the fracture in the realm's harmony.

"She is… gone," murmured Avat'or, his eyes hardening. "The Hrothgorn loyalists… it is revenge. Draknorr's followers have struck at the heart of Tyr."

The council of Arom gathered the weight of leadership heavy upon them. They had been chosen by the Destiny of Tyr to guide the world in Dragonwülf's stead, yet none of their training could prepare them for the sudden, violent absence of the Queen who had held their world together.

A flicker of light—a vision, or perhaps the will of the Destiny itself— appeared before them. Valkyrja's voice, soft but unwavering, whispered through the minds of those gathered:

"Do not let grief cloud your purpose. I have lived as Valorii, as Valkyrja, and I leave you the courage to carry on. The world will bend… but it will not break."

Dragonwülf's jaw tightened. "Then we act," he said, his voice cutting through the haze of despair. "The Hrothgorn cannot go unchallenged. Their vengeance has left Arom vulnerable, and the world will bleed if we hesitate."

Svean's hands trembled as he gripped the edge of the table. "But… the queen…her death has shifted the balance. The Destinies… they stir. We feel it, do we not?"

"Yes," Dragonwülf replied. "The balance is fractured. The void left by her passing calls to those who would feast upon it. We must be swift. We must be relentless."

Outside, the city stirred. The assassins had vanished like shadows, leaving no trace beyond their act of terror. Whispers of Valkyrja's death would spread like wildfire, sowing fear among the people and those who coveted power.

Dragonwülf lifted his gaze toward the heavens, toward the unseen watchers of the Destiny of Tyr. "We will not fail her," he vowed. "I will stand. We will stand. And those who struck in darkness… they will answer."

Morning Fire of the Sky unfurled her wings, a silent promise of fury and fire. Below, the city of Arom awoke, unaware that a war had begun not just in its streets, but also in the hearts and fates of all who lived under the shadow of the Queen's passing.

"*I will avenge thee, my Queen and my friend*, vowed Dragonwülf. "The Hrothgorn will pay for their evil deed, I swear it."

The echoes of Valkyrja's life lingered in the air, a call to arms, a warning, and a promise: the balance may be broken, but from its shards, a greater reckoning would rise.

And in the quiet corners of the Kingdom, a faint shimmer of light—almost like a heartbeat—hinted that Destiny was already stirring, preparing the threads of vengeance and triumph for the days to come.

The Day of Queen Valkyrja
128 BCE Kingdom of Arom

Her Majesty the Queen, first of her name, was laid to rest in a plain stone tomb for all eternity. These words were spoken by the elders of the Kingdom.

"Queen Valkyrja was a beacon in a world of shadow, her wisdom a guiding star for all who sought justice and honor. She ruled not with fear, but with courage and compassion, teaching us that true strength is measured not in the power we wield, but in the lives we uplift. Though her voice is now silent, her spirit endures, echoing in the hearts of those who remember her deeds and carry forth her legacy."

"Drottning Valkyrja var ljós í heimi myrkurs, viska hennar stjörnu leiðbeining fyrir alla sem leituðu réttlætis ok heiðurs. Hún réð eigi með ótta, heldr með hugrekki ok samkennd, kenndi oss at sönn styrkr mátast eigi í valdi sem vér höfum, heldr í lífum sem vér lyftum. Þó at rødd hennar er nú þögul, andar hennar lifa, bergmál í hjörtum þeirra sem minnast verka hennar ok bera áfram arf hennar."

These are the images engraved on her tomb.

"Hér hvílir Valkyrja, drottning drengja,
ljós í myrkri, stjarna visku.
Hugr ok réttlæti fylgdu henni,
ekki vald eða ótti heldur hjarta og sverð.
Sterk hún stóð í stormum,
mild í friði, réttlát með alla.
Hún lifir enn í sálum þeirra
sem minnast verk hennar ok bera arf hennar áfram.
Rødd hennar þögul, en kraftur hennar ódauðr,
eins og eldur sem lýsir nótt ok leiðir vegferð manna."

Here rests Valkyrja, Queen of the brave,
light in darkness, star of wisdom.
Courage and justice followed her,
not power or fear, but heart and sword.

Strong she stood in storms,

gentle in peace, just with all.

She still lives in the souls.

of those who remember her deeds and carry her legacy onward.

Her voice is silent, but her strength is undying,

like a fire that lights the night and guides men's journey."

Artifact Twenty

Light at the Edge of the World

Date: Dimension of Róthul-Orkr 2018 CE
Atlantic Ocean near Newfoundland and
(Near The Undersea of Morak)

L'appel Du Vide (The Call of the Void)
- An overwhelming urge to hurl oneself into the abyss.

The wind whispered through the trees, carrying with it a sense of mystery and allure. A group of sea island cliff dwellers stood at the edge of a cliff overlooking the vast expanse of the ocean below. The waves crashed against the rocks, creating a symphony of sound that echoed in their ears.

One of them, Vigdis, turned to her friends with a glint of excitement in her eyes. "I have always wondered what it would be like to venture into the depths of the ocean," she mused. "I want to feel the water surrounding me, embracing me as if it were destiny. I just want to be submerged for a while."

Her friend Sigurvaldi chuckled, "Have you lost your mind? Are you suggesting we just jump in for no good reason?" His voice was tinged with a mix of curiosity and apprehension.

As they pondered the idea, the sun began to set, casting a golden hue over the water. The scene was mesmerizing, the perfect water shimmering like a blanket of diamonds.

With a shared glance, the two made their decision. Together, they descended the cliff and entered the cool embrace of the ocean. The water enveloped them, its touch both chilling and comforting.

As they swam deeper, the world above faded away, replaced by a surreal dreamscape of swirling currents and dancing light. Vigdis's heart raced with a mix of fear and exhilaration, the perfect water guiding them further into the unknown. The undertow became all too powerful as they marveled at the dancing lights below.

Both Sigurvaldi and Vigdis were then violently pulled beneath the surface of the ocean. As Vigdis was pulled under the water, she held her breath in the hope that she might resurface and recover her breath. It was not meant to be. She allowed the cold Atlantic to enter her lungs as her body sank to the floor of the sea.

Vigdis and Sigurvaldi had always shared a deep sense of adventure. Nothing could have prepared them for the fateful day they found themselves lost at sea, drifting in the vastness of the Atlantic Ocean. As the waves crashed around them, pulling them under, they held onto each other for dear life, their lungs burning for air.

In a miraculous twist of fate, instead of succumbing to the darkness of the deep, they found themselves sinking further into the ocean depths, their bodies weightless as they descended into the unknown.

"Could this be a dream?" she gasped, her voice filled with awe as she reached out to touch a passing school of shimmering fish.

Sigurvaldi, his face a mix of fear and wonder, could only shake his head in disbelief.

As they continued to sink deeper, a majestic shadow loomed before them, causing Vigdis and Sigurvaldi to freeze in awe. The massive figure of Róthul-Orkr, the whale God, swam gracefully towards them, his voice resonating in their minds.

"Welcome, travelers," Róthul-Orkr boomed, his presence awe-inspiring yet serene. "You have been brought here for a purpose, to witness the beauty and wisdom of the underwater realm."

Vigdis and John Sigurvaldi exchanged wide-eyed glances, their hearts racing with a mixture of fear and excitement.

"What do you mean?" Vigdis stammered her voice barely above a whisper.

The Whale God's eyes glowed with ancient wisdom as he spoke, his words reverberating through the water around them. "The ocean holds the secrets of the universe, the ebb and flow of life itself. You have been granted this rare opportunity to glimpse its wonders and understand the interconnectedness of all living beings."

The sea friends listened in rapt attention as Róthul-Orkr shared tales of sunken cities and forgotten civilizations, of creatures beyond imagination and mysteries waiting to be unraveled. They marveled at the intricate beauty of the underwater architecture, the intricate dance of the fish, and the boundless expanse of the sea.

As the whale God's words washed over them like a gentle tide, Vigdis and Sigurvaldi felt a profound sense of peace settling within their souls. They realized that in the vastness of the ocean, they were but small specks in a grand tapestry of life, connected to every living creature in ways they had never imagined.

As they drifted deeper into the heart of the ocean, the sea creatures embraced the mysteries that surrounded them, their spirits forever changed by the wisdom of Róthul-Orkr and the boundless wonders of the deep. Beneath the waves of the Atlantic Ocean, they found not only answers but also a newfound sense of purpose and a connection that transcended time and space.

In the depths, they encountered wonders beyond imagination - schools of colorful fish, coral reefs teeming with life, and underwater caves shrouded in mystery. They marveled at the beauty that surrounded them, feeling a deep connection to the heart of the ocean.

As they dove deeper, a sense of peace washed over them, like a warm embrace from the sea itself.

In that moment, beneath the waves, they understood the true meaning of freedom and adventure. In the embrace of water, they found a sense of unity with each other and the vast expanse of the ocean.

Suddenly, a loud splash interrupted their conversation. They turned to see a group of dolphins playing in the distance, their joyful calls echoing through the air as they swam playfully.

Vigdis and Sigurvaldi found themselves navigating the depths of the sea in the company of Róthul-Orkr, a wise and ancient whale who had taken them under his fin. As they swam gracefully through the sunken world beneath the waves, they marveled at the beauty and wonder that surrounded them.

"Look there," Vigdis exclaimed, pointing towards a distant shadow looming in the murky depths. "Is that what I think it is?"

Sigurvaldi squinted his eyes and followed her gaze, his heart quickening with excitement. "A sunken Spanish galleon!" he gasped, his voice muffled by the water. "Let us go and explore!"

Róthul-Orkr nodded sagely, leading the way toward the ancient shipwreck. As they drew closer, they could see the remains of the grand vessel, its timbers encrusted with coral and its cannons long silenced.

Suddenly, a ghostly figure emerged from the shadows of the wreck. It was Captain Drekar, his spectral form clad in tattered rags and his eyes burning with a fierce light.

"Who dares to intrude upon my domain?" Captain Drekar boomed, his voice echoing through the water.

"We mean no harm, Captain," Vigdis spoke up, her voice strong and clear. "We are merely travelers seeking to learn the secrets of the deep."

Captain Drekar regarded them with a suspicious eye, but then a sly grin crossed his face. "Travelers, you say? Very well, come closer, and I shall show you something that will chill your very souls."

As they followed Captain Drekar into the heart of the wreck, they came upon a scene of horror and betrayal. The crew of "The Fjordcutter" lay scattered around with their bones picked clean by the creatures of the deep. In the center of it all was the figure of Captain Drekar himself, tied to the mainsail with ropes of seaweed.

"The crew mutinied against me," Captain Drekar explained bitterly, his voice heavy with regret. "They plotted against me and left me here to die. But I swore that I would never rest until I had my revenge."

The sea dwellers listened in awe as Captain Drekar recounted the tale of the ill-fated voyage of The Fjordcutter. The ship had been caught in a terrible storm, and the crew, driven mad by fear and greed, had turned against their captain in a bid for power.

"So here I remain, bound to this sunken wreck for all eternity," Captain Drekar concluded, his voice fading into a ghostly whisper. "Perhaps with your help, I may yet find

"It is through the cleansing of the sea that we become perfected and step into the realm of godhood. What is the sea to the Destiny of Tyr? Is it homage to Róthul-Orkr? Are the shipwrecks that lie with broken spines on the bottom of the sea the former vessels of these gods? Why is the entire Destiny born of the sea? It is simple. The souls who pass through the Destiny of Tyr are born of the water to begin a new life, to right the wrongs of the past, and to begin again.

Róthul-Orkr floated just beneath the surface of the sea, his weathered face bathed in the golden light of the setting sun. His gaze was fixed on the horizon, where the endless expanse of the sea met the sky in a breathtaking display of colors. The sea winds parted the water as he pondered the mysteries of the tempest-tossed island that lay just beyond his reach. Once again, as he had done for all of eternity, The Whale-God set fire to the beacon at the end of the world.

As he watched wave upon wave crash against the rocky shore, a voice called out to him from beneath. It was Old Captain Drekar and his ghost ship, The Fjordcutter. The Captain's eyes were wide with wonder as he took in the scene before him. "Excuse me, Your Majesty…uh, your whale *holiness* or…Uh, I am sorry. I do not know how to address you," he began tentatively, "but I couldn't help but notice you are here in person… or in whale-ness… I am sorry. I am in awe of you. Until this time, I was not sure you even existed."

The Whale turned to face the Captain, a knowing smile playing on his lips. "Aye, I come here every evening to watch the sun sink below the horizon and light the way for those lost at sea," he replied in a voice that carried the weight of years spent in solitude. "It's a sight that never fails to stir the soul."

The Captain nodded, his curiosity piqued by Róthul-Orkr's words. "Tell me, Whale King," I know that you light the beacon at the end of the world every night. What purpose does it serve?" he asked, eager to unravel the mystery that shrouded the nightly ritual.

Orca's eyes sparkled with a pearl of ancient wisdom as he regarded the old Captain.

"The beacon serves as a guiding light for those who are far from home, lost in the vastness of the sea," he explained. "It offers hope to weary travelers, a glimmer of light in the darkness that leads them safely back to shore."

"But why do you do it, my King? What drives you to swim here each night, watching over the sea like a guardian?" The Captain pressed on, his voice tinged with awe and admiration for the ancient Whale's selfless dedication.

The Orca chuckled softly, his gaze drifting back to the horizon where the first stars began to twinkle in the twilight sky. "I do it because once, long ago, I was the one lost at sea, adrift and alone with no hope of finding my way home," he confessed, his voice filled with emotion." I light the beacon to pay homage to the light that guided me back to safety, to ensure that others may find their way as I once did. That is my duty as a sea God. I must light the way for others to find their way in the dark."

Artifact Twenty- One

Cyrus the Pretender

Date: Dimension of Thor (2421 CE)
The United States of AmeriKa, Earth

"I am the champion of the people," he boasted with bloated cheeks.
"They love me."

The night was draped in darkness, the moon shy to reveal its radiance as the kingdom of AmeriKa slept under a blanket of fear. A chilling wind whispered through the asphalt-paved streets. At the heart of it all, perched upon a throne of deception, sat the vile king of lies, President Cyrus Kain. The former United States of America was now a pile of ruins. America was a slag pile of broken promises, shattered dreams, and ruined lives.

In the middle of it all was President Kain, his crown gleaming with false majesty, each twisted gem a testament to the treachery that pulsed within his black heart. The people whispered tales of his cruelty, of the lives he had shattered in his insatiable quest for power. Yet, like a puppet on a string, he danced to the tune of his own madness, blind to the suffering he caused.

"I am the champion of the people," he bellowed, his voice dripping with honeyed lies. "I am the savior of this broken world, forged in the fire of my own people. They love me, they really do." His words hung in the air like a poisonous fog, clouding the minds of those who dared to listen.

Not all were fooled by his false face. In the shadows, a rebel alliance plotted their uprising, their whispers a symphony of defiance against the tyrant king. "It is time to dethrone him," they vowed, their eyes alight with the fire of rebellion. "It is time to end his reign of terror and restore justice to our land."

President Kain, a man once revered for his promises of change and unity, now ruled with an iron fist. His thirst for power and control knew no bounds, and the citizens of the newly renamed AmeriKa, at the insistence of her new president, lived in fear and oppression.

In the heart of the bustling city of Washington, D.C., a dark shadow loomed over the nation as Cyrus Kain was sworn in as the new President of the United States of America. With his charismatic smile and silver tongue, he captured the hearts of the American people, promising a new era of prosperity and unity. Little did they know, behind closed doors, Kain harbored a sinister agenda that would shake the foundations of the country.

As the days turned into weeks, whispers of corruption and greed began to circulate within the hallowed halls of the White House. Kain's true colors started to reveal themselves as he made backroom deals with corporate giants, sacrificing the welfare of the people for his own personal gain.

"I'll make sure you get that defense contract, just wire the money to this offshore account," he chuckled darkly into the phone, his eyes glinting with malice.

Meanwhile, protests erupted in the streets as citizens demanded transparency and accountability from their leaders. However, the President's wrath came down hard on dissenters, using the full force of his power to crush any hint of rebellion.

"You elected me to do this!" his voice boomed through the halls of the Capitol, his face twisted into a menacing sneer. "You will all pay dearly for your disrespect. I am only doing what I was put here to do."

Underneath his charming facade, Cyrus Kain's insatiable thirst for power knew no bounds. He manipulated the media, silencing any voice that dared to speak out against him. His propaganda machine worked tirelessly to brainwash the masses, painting him as a savior while demonizing his opponents.

"I am the chosen one, the one who will lead this country to greatness," Kain declared to a crowd of cheering supporters, his eyes ablaze with madness. "The others are lesser than us!"

As the days turned into months, the once-great nation of America descended into chaos and despair under the King's tyrannical rule. His evil deeds knew no limits as he trampled over their Constitution, eradicating any semblance of democracy in his quest for absolute power.

"Someday, and it will be soon, I will press the button that will bring missiles to bear on the earth. There will be war, death, and victory for me! I will rule the earth, and none will be left except those I protect. All will bow down," Kain wrote in his Presidential log. "The people put me here to rid the world of vermin, and I will do just that!

In the end, it was not a hero who brought Kain to his knees, but the very darkness he had unleashed upon the world. He would soon suffer the same blindness and darkness.

⚬⚬◆⚬⚬

The Deepwater Watchman found a portal to this time to attempt an intervention. The Harvester of Eyes would soon meet President Cyrus Kain.

"This man must be stopped," said Dragonwülf. You must face him. We cannot return to the ancient of days to avenge our Queen until we meet this present evil face to face. I thirst for the blood of the Hrothgorn for the death of our Queen, but I know I must be patient. You will meet evil on Earth today.

This man rages with fury and must be made to see that he has been manipulated by the Defiler of Souls."

"Why am I to be sent to do this?" asked Gru'el.

"The same level of evil that is within Kain is also within you. None among us can see that as you," explained Dragonwülf.

"I am blind, you fool, and I have no eyes except those I collect."

"Precisely, old man, you see the evil in men's souls clearer than any of us. He must be stopped, even if it means a sacrifice of your life."

"Why would I need to sacrifice? I have also been promised immortality by the Destiny of Tyr," said Gru'el, quite aggravated.

"Yes, but you must reconcile the evil you have done by experiencing Kain's evil. If you fail, you will die. This is the only way to destroy the evil within you. Let us face the facts, old man. You are very evil," said Dragonwülf. "I exiled you on the Isle of Kelda for a good reason."

Gru'el thought for a moment and spoke. "Very well, I will go and do this. If it takes a sacrifice on my part, I will do it. My life has been filled with evil deeds and unspeakable acts, and I simply tire of them."

In a flash of blinding light, Han'sel Gru'el, Viktor Vorobyev, and Luciano Cantore were transported outside the President's bedchamber of the White House, now renamed the House of Kain. In the dimly lit room, the Harvester of Eyes loomed over President Cyrus Kain, a sinister aura enveloping him like a cloak of shadows. The Harvesters' three companions captured and bound the three secret service officers. Bound to a chair, Kain stared defiantly at the masked figure before him. The Harvester's jet-black cloak billowed ominously, its hood casting a veil of darkness over his face; save for his piercing eyes that glowed with an otherworldly intensity.

"You will pay for your crimes," the Harvester's voice echoed in the room, sending shivers down the spines of Kain and his men who stood guard around him.

Kain sneered, his arrogance shining through despite the dire situation. "You think you can stop me, you masked freak? I am the rightful leader of this nation, and nothing will stand in my way. The people love me! Just ask anyone, they will tell you."

"My name is Hansel Gru'el, and I am known as The Harvester of Eyes. I can see all you do and all you have done and even what you are thinking by taking your eyes and looking through them."

"I thought I was twisted and evil, which I am… but this? You win the evil reward today."

"The only reason your eyeball is not in my head at this very moment is that I have been told by someone wiser that there may be redemption for you yet. I have someone who would like to speak with you," said the Harvester.

"I have no need to talk! Do what you will and do it fast!" bellowed Kain.

The double doors of the bedchamber opened slowly and stately as a ghost entered Abraham Lincoln.

"Good evening, Mr. Kain."

"Am I supposed to believe you are actually Abe Lincoln? Don't be preposterous, you old fool!" said Kain.

"I assure you, Sir, that I am indeed him," said Lincoln. These men with me are my shipmates, and we have been sent with a task to undo evil wherever we see it."

"Suppose you are telling the truth? What good would it do me?" asked Kain.

"Listen to me, Cyrus," said Lincoln softly. I know who you are because I have been where you are and I have held the office of President."

"We are not the same. I have brought my people together, and you caused a Civil war."

I faced the same challenge as you did early in my presidency. I was offered payoffs, bribes if you will, to do or not to do certain things just as you have," said Lincoln. "I would have been rich beyond my dreams, and I would have lived out my many days with riches with my family."

"I would have taken a deal," said Kain. "That just makes you foolish."

"No, that just makes me free. If I had taken such money, it would have cost my soul."

"I also could no longer sit idly by and watch the torture and ownership of men, women, and children under my watch, and I paid for it with a bullet in the head."

"That was because there were people who hated you… If I read my history correctly," said Kain.

"*Your people,* as you call them, do not love you; they fear you," said Lincoln. "Do not suppose otherwise. You still have time to listen to reason. The Harvester's hands are idle, but he does not do well when he is bored."

"I do not believe in redemption, repentance, or any of their brothers and sisters. Go to Hell!" bellowed Kain.

Without a word, the Harvester approached Kain with eerie calmness, his gloved hands reaching out to grasp the President's head. In one swift motion, he dug his fingers into Kain's eye socket, causing a gut-wrenching scream to fill the room. The sound of tearing flesh and cracking bone reverberated off the walls as the Harvester ripped the eye and socket from Kain's skull, a grotesque trophy of his victory.

"This did not have to be done!" cried President Lincoln. "I would have opened a dialogue with him! I just needed more time!"

As the President writhed in agony, his men tried to move to intervene, but the Harvester was quicker than they could react. Gru'el stuffed the eyeball into his own hollow socket. With lightning speed, he dispatched each guard with a deadly precision that left no room for mercy. The room descended into chaos as the Harvester moved with fluidity that defied human capabilities, his every movement calculated and deadly as he removed the eyeballs of the guards as well. Shrieks of fear and agony filled the West Wing, as well as groans of "Oh my God, why is he doing this?" He stuffed his newly obtained treasure into his bag, latched to his ghoulish belt. The sound of gunfire and loud thuds came from outside the chamber as the Secret Service tried to gain entry. Gru'el had pre-planned.

"I am the Harvester of Eyes!" said Gru'el. "This is what I do. It would be presumptuous for you to suppose otherwise."

"You are a ghoulish freak and a lunatic!" howled Kain through his newfound pain.

"You are nothing but a puppet, Kain," the Harvester spoke with a chilling finality as he loomed over the fallen leader. "AmeriKa will rise from the ashes, free from your tyranny. Tell me who pays you? I swear upon all that you cherish, I will have your other eye as well, Kain. Who pulls your strings?"

With one last look of defiance, President Cyrus Kain spat in the face of the Harvester and drew his final breath.

"Rest well in the halls of Hades," said Gru'el, as he looked upon the twisted face of the former dictator.

The Harvester of Eyes was soon to vanish into the shadows, leaving behind a legacy of fear and liberation in his wake. President Lincoln was left standing over the dying body of President Kain as he said a small prayer for the now former president.

"Thou knowest his works, his designs, and the suffering wrought by his hand. Nothing is hidden from Thine eternal judgment, and justice is Thine to mete, not mine to speak. Yet as I stand among the living, I pray that his

passing may close the book of cruelty and open, in its stead, a page of repentance beyond the veil."

Before the President passed into oblivion, Lincoln thought he heard Kain speak the name "Pollutore Animarum."

The Harvester before the Council of Gods

In an instant, the sun began to set, painting the sky in vibrant hues of orange and pink. Hansel Gru'el found himself transported from the office of Cyrus Kain to standing at the entrance to the grand hall where the council of gods awaited him. The imposing marble pillars marked his path as he walked toward the judgment that awaited him. The Gods had ordered the Harvester to appear before them to answer for his crimes against humanity. The good that he had done with Dragonwülf and the Destiny of Tyr may not have been enough to balance his crimes.

Upon entering the hall, Hansel was met with a breathtaking sight. The council of gods sat upon golden thrones, their shimmering robes billowing behind them. The panel of deities exuded power and authority, their eyes fixed on the figure standing before them.

"Loki, god of mischief and trickery, your presence is requested to oversee the trial of Hansel Gru'el," boomed Óðinn, the All-Father.

Hansel's heart pounded in his chest as Loki appeared beside him, his emerald eyes gleaming with a mischievous glint. Loki's lips curled into a sly smile as he whispered, "Don't worry, mortal. I've always had a soft spot for those who defy both gods and men."

Hansel knew that his fate hung in the balance as the council of gods began to speak. Each deity recounted the atrocities committed by Hansel, the Harvester of Eyes. They spoke of the cities he had left in ruins, the populations he had left trembling in fear.

As the trial went on, a different narrative began to emerge. The council heard of how Hansel had turned the tables on the evil President and Dictator Cyrus Kain, saving AmeriKa from his tyrannical rule. They heard of how he had promised to sacrifice all to protect the innocent, even at the cost of his own life.

The god of weapons and war, Tyr, spoke in a dark tone.

"You have walked a dark path, mortal," he began, his voice echoing through the hall. "But in doing so, you have brought light to those who needed it most. For your bravery and sacrifice, we offer you a chance at redemption."

Hansel's eyes widened in disbelief as the council of gods offered him a choice. He could accept banishment from the realm of gods and men, never to return. He could join their ranks as a protector of the innocent, forever bound by duty and honor.

With a steely resolve, Hansel made his choice. "I will stand as a guardian of the realm," he declared, his voice unwavering. "I will use my skills to protect the innocent and uphold justice, no matter the cost."

Hansel Gru'el was granted mercy by the council of gods. With a new purpose and a new destiny, he strode out of the grand hall, his past sins behind him. As the doors closed behind him, a new legend began to take shape - the story of a man who had committed some of the darkest acts in history but emerged as a hero in the eyes of gods and men alike.

Artifact Twenty- Two

The Death of the Deepwater

fall dauðans djúps

ᚤᚠᚱ ᛗᚠᚢᛈᚠᛏᛊ ᛗᛂᛈᚳᛊ

Date: Future Dimension of Höðr (2296 CE)

"I wish that time would freeze in place and the gods would forget about
me and go about their business.
I have no wish for the passage of time."
– Captain Old Turas

Amid a tumultuous storm, the crew of the illustrious ship Deepwater
Watchman found themselves battling against the unrelenting fury of outer

space. Captain Old-Turas stood at the helm, his grip tight on the wheel as he regaled his crew with tales.

"Let me tell you of a tale of a brave soldier who fought with me on the day of the battle of Harvest Moon. Tor'Bjorn the shoemaker fought with fury against the Hrothgorn and their demons. He never returned when the battle was done. Some say he destroyed the Palace of Bones by burning it to the ground. We never found him. Some say he still fights with the righteous spirits to this day. Some others say his soul lives on in all soldiers who fight against evil. What we know is that we would never have found King Draknorr and his prisoners otherwise."

The clipper ship glided through the vast expanse of space, its sails unfurled and catching the cosmic winds. Aboard the ship, Old Captain Turas paced back and forth, his weathered face etched with determination. Luciano Cantore leaned against the railing, a glint of mischief in his eyes. Viktor Vorobyev, a rugged member of a biker gang, sat cross-legged on the deck, his arms crossed over his chest. Jarvis Nightwish stood in quiet contemplation by the ship's helm. Sir Robert Winterfall poured over a dusty map in the dim light below deck. Zachariah Boyd twirled his pistols with practiced ease, a smirk playing on his lips.

As the ship sailed through the star-studded skies, a mysterious force guided them toward their destination, the floating city of Tyr. Legends spoke of Tyr as the realm where destiny itself resided, and it was said that only the elite were granted an audience with the enigmatic being that ruled over the city.

Old Captain Turas gathered the group on the deck, his voice booming with authority. "We have been summoned to Tyr by the hands of fate itself," he declared, his gaze sweeping over his companions. "Each of us bears a legacy of our own, but together, we possess the strength to face whatever awaits us in that fabled city."

Luciano Cantore chuckled softly, flicking a stray piece of lint off his tailored suit. "I ain't one for destiny and all that jazz, but I reckon a little adventure wouldn't hurt," he remarked, his eyes glinting with intrigue.

Viktor Vorobyev grunted in agreement, his fingers tracing the intricate tattoos that adorned his arms. "I have faced many challenges in my life, but this... this feels different," he mused, his gaze fixed on the horizon.

Jarvis Nightwish remained silent, his piercing gaze fixed on the distant lights of the Destiny of Tyr. The executioner was known for his stoic demeanor, his origins shrouded in mystery. "Destiny is but a path we must walk," he spoke at last, his voice as cold as the void of space.

Zachariah Boyd holstered his pistols with a grin, the sun glinting off the barrels. "Well, I ain't one to turn down a good fight," he drawled, his cowboy hat casting a shadow over his rugged features.

The unlikely band of companions sailed towards Tyr, their destinies intertwined by a greater force. What awaited them in the floating city of fate was a mystery yet to be unraveled, but one thing was certain. This journey would test their courage, their strength, and their bonds of friendship like never before.

"We must stay the course, lads!" he bellowed over the howling winds. "Hold fast to the mast and brace you!"

As the outer space realm storm raged on, the Deep Water Watchman was tossed about like a mere toy in the hands of a mischievous giant. The wind in space crashed against the sides of the ship, threatening to pull it down at any moment.

"We're starting to lilt the starboard side, Captain!" shouted his first mate, his voice filled with urgency. "We can't hold her much longer!"

Captain Turas' jaw clenched in determination. Space showed no mercy. The Deepwater Watchman died the way only old ships do—slowly at first, with indignity, then all at once.

The windstorm came without a horizon. Space should have been empty, but the storm had mass, a river of charged particles and gravitic shear spilling out of a collapsed stellar wake. It struck the *Watchman* broadside like an ocean squall hitting a wooden hull, invisible yet overwhelming, screaming across the void with the pressure of a god exhaling.

Captain Santiago Old-Turas felt it before the alarms.

The deck beneath his boots shuddered. It was not a clean vibration, but a sick, rolling tremor, like a spine trying to remember how to bend.

"Helm," he said calmly, gripping the brass rail bolted into the command dais. "Report."

The reply never came.

The forward viewplate warped, stars smearing into long, white scars as the ship's inertial compensators lagged a heartbeat behind reality. The Deepwater groaned, a deep, structural moan that traveled the length of her keel. She had been built for pressure and patience. She was built for long hauls, deep voids, but this was not pressure. This was *directional violence*.

The first thing to go was the sail array.

Not torn away—*peeled*.

The solar vanes flexed past tolerance, folding backward as wings snapped at the joint. Superstructure spars shrieked as molecular bonds failed, and then the sails shattered into a glittering cloud of fractured light, spinning away into the storm like dying birds.

"Captain!" the navigator finally cried, voice breaking through the static. "We're caught in a shear—gravitic vectors are—"

Old-Turas didn't flinch. He had lost crews before. Panic was a contagion; calm was armor.

"Seal the mid-decks," he ordered to no one in particular. "Dump mass. Jettison the port ballast."

The storm twisted, and The Watchman yawed hard to starboard, her ancient frame fighting forces it had never been designed to name. Internal bulkheads buckled. Somewhere deep in the ship, a corridor collapsed, steel folding like wet paper, crushing airlocks and men alike in silence no vacuum could hear.

The engine core flared. Not an explosion…yet…but a furious, caged sun suddenly exposed to the storm's appetite. Power conduits ruptured, arcing blue lightning through engineering bays. Gravity inverted twice in three seconds, slamming crew into ceilings, then floors, then walls, leaving bodies broken in corners as the ship struggled to remember which way was *down*.

Old-Turas was thrown from his feet.

He hit the deck hard, breath driven from his lungs, blood blooming warm at his temple. Still, he pushed himself up, one hand braced against the helm console as the bridge lights flickered to a funereal red.

"Old girl," he muttered, voice low and intimate, as if speaking to a wounded animal. "You've carried me far enough."

The storm found the keel.

A pressure wave rippled along the ship's spine, compressing and releasing metal faster than it could adapt. Rivets sheared free. Structural ribs cracked. The *Deepwater Watchman* bent—*bent*—her proud, elongated hull bowing into a slow, terrible arc.

"Captain," a young voice whispered over an open channel, barely audible. "We're breaking apart."

Old-Turas closed his eyes for half a second.

"I know," he said. "You did well."

The bridge canopy imploded.

Transparent alloy spiderwebbed, then vanished inward as the storm punched through. Atmosphere screamed out in a white, furious torrent, ripping consoles from their moorings, tearing crew from handholds. Old-Turas was lifted, weightless, his coat snapping like a banner as stars rushed toward him.

The ship split at midship.

Not cleanly. Nothing about it was clean.

The bow section twisted away, still burning, still trying to fly. The aft compartments lagged behind, and the engine core was overloading. Between them stretched a moment of impossible tension, a single, frozen heartbeat where the ship seemed to hesitate, deciding whether to die as one.

Then the storm answered for her.

The engine core ruptured.

Light swallowed the wreckage—not a flash, but a blooming, expanding sphere of annihilation, folding metal, memory, and name into incandescent debris. Fragments of the Watchman were flung outward, tumbling end over end, glowing like embers cast into a cosmic gale.

Captain Santiago Old-Turas never screamed.

He drifted, silhouetted against the dying fire of his ship, eyes open, watching the remains scatter across the dark like the last chapter of a long voyage written in shrapnel and flame.

For a brief, impossible instant, the storm carried him gently.

Then even that mercy was gone.

With a deafening crack, the Deep Water Watchman splintered in two, dropping from outer space, sending its crew tumbling into the icy embrace of the atmosphere below. Amidst the chaos, cries for help rose up into the stormy night, mingling with the sound of thunder and crashing winds as the ship tumbled to the earth and sea below.

As the ship sank beneath the churning waters, the crew found themselves clinging to whatever debris they could find. In the midst of it all, the Captain's voice cut through the chaos.

"Stay together, my friends!" he called out, his words carrying above the howling wind. "We may be battered, but we are not beaten! We will fight on, for as long as we draw breath!"

In their darkest hour, the crew of the Deep Water Watchman forged a bond stronger than any tempest. As they struggled to stay afloat in the unforgiving sea, they shared stories of distant lands, of loves lost, and of dreams yet to be fulfilled.

As the minutes turned into hours, hope began to wane. The crew grew weary, their bodies weakened by exposure and hunger. One by one, they slipped beneath the waves, their voices silenced by the depths of the ocean.

In the end, only Captain Turas and Dragonwülf remained, their gazes locked in a silent understanding. Together, they watched as the sun dipped below the horizon, painting the sky in hues of orange and gold.

"Meet me on the other side, my friend. I will wait on the shore for you.

As one, they descended into the watery depths, their souls bound together by the unbreakable ties of camaraderie and courage.

The crew of the Deep Water Watchman met their final destiny, their names forever etched in the annals of maritime history as brave souls who faced the perils of the sea with unwavering resolve.

As members of the Deepwater Watchman drifted ashore, their bloated bodies covered in seaweed, Avat'or stood with his gaze fixed upon the horizon. The salty breeze carried whispers of ancient tales, and the crashing waves sang a lullaby of forgotten legends.

"It is the sea from which we draw our strength," Avat'or declared, his voice as deep and powerful as the ocean itself. "And it is from the sea we draw life from death. These members of the crew of the Deepwater Watchman shall once again live! Hear the words of my mouth. *This is not a prayer. This is a command to the crew*. Come forth!"

———✦———

For centuries, the council held the knowledge and wisdom of life and death of the oceans, guiding the balance beneath the waves. Their connection to the sea had bestowed incredible abilities upon them to harness its power, granting them the ability to manipulate currents, communicate with marine creatures, and even control the weather.

The origins of the Destiny of Tyr can be traced back to a time long forgotten. Legend speaks of a mighty sea deity named Róthul-Orkr, known for his benevolence and unwavering dedication to protecting the oceanic realm. Róthul-Orkr had chosen mortal champions who were born of the sea, imbuing them with extraordinary gifts to safeguard the natural wonders hidden beneath the waves.

The chosen members dedicated their lives to studying the oceans and ensuring harmony with the ever-changing tides.

Yet, questions lingered within the council. Why were they to be born on the sea? What significance did it hold? Secrets long held in silence were finally unveiled during a momentous assembly of the Destiny of Tyr.

Now Dragonwülf and the crew of the Deepwater were seated in a grand hall adorned with sea-inspired tapestries and shimmering crystals. Destiny of Tyr members from all corners of the sea and earth convened. The air crackled with an electric anticipation. It was time for the council to reveal the truth behind their ancestry.

As the council's eldest member rose to address the gathering, the room fell into a hushed silence. His voice, weathered by age, carried an air of wisdom. He spoke of an ancient prophecy, hidden within the depths of the seas, foretelling a time when humanity would face its greatest crisis, an impending threat that could unravel the fabric of existence.

"Just one moment if you please," asked Dragonwülf. Where are we? How did we all end up here?"

"This is the grand hall of the seas. This is the beginning of life. We are in the seat of all beginnings."

"Who are you that you would bring us here?" asked Old-Turas.

"My name is no matter to anyone. I have not heard it uttered in one thousand years. I will likely never hear it. It is the sea from which we draw our strength," he began, his words resonating through the hearts of all who listened. "We are bound to the ocean, for it is within its depths that our true destiny lies." He further explained that the Destiny of Tyr had been entrusted with the task of safeguarding an artifact known as the Urn of the Dead Gods. This ancient relic, forged from the soul of Tyr himself, held the power to ward off the impending darkness and bring balance to the world.

Each member of the council bore a fragment of the Urn of the Dead Gods within their very being, a connection to the divine power that was granted at birth. The sea, being the cradle of life, was thus intertwined with their existence. Only through their unique bond with the ocean could the council channel the full extent of their abilities and safeguard the fragments of the Urn from falling into the wrong hands.

With this revelation, the council understood the true gravity of their purpose. Their ancestry was not a mere coincidence but a deliberate design to ensure the survival of all life. They were the guardians, the protectors of the delicate balance of the world, and the last line of defense against the encroaching darkness.

The Destiny of Tyr became a beacon of hope, their legacy etched into the annals of time. Legends were born, and the council's tale was passed down through generations, inspiring future protectors of the ocean.

As the tide continues to ebb and flow, the Destiny of Tyr endures, their connection to the sea driving their purpose. Born of the ocean, their destiny is intertwined with its very essence, forever binding them to a sacred duty, a duty to protect all within the realm. The pieces of the Urn would be passed on to a new generation of the Destiny of Tyr.

Enter the new era of the new members of the Destiny of Tyr.

Artifact Twenty -Three

Dragonwülf's Council of Tyr

Date: Future Dimension of Thor (2229 CE)

**"Although I wish for more trips around the moon
And one more dance upon the sea,
I know I have seen all there is to see. I can dream no more."**

In the great halls of Valhalla, Dragonwülf stood before the council of the Destiny, a group of powerful beings who had chosen him to be the protector of the earthen realm. His dragon companion, The Morning Fire of the Sky, stood proudly beside him, its scales gleaming in the dim light of the hall.

"We have bestowed upon you the armor of titanium, forged by the gods themselves," Father Óðinn spoke in a voice that boomed through the hall. "With this armor, no blade shall pierce your skin, and no fire shall burn you."

Dragonwülf bowed his head in gratitude, feeling the weight of his new responsibility settling on his shoulders. "I will not fail you, my Lords. I will protect the realm with all that I have."

The council nodded in approval, and Frigg, the goddess of destiny, stepped forward, her eyes filled with ancient wisdom. "We have also outfitted you with modern weapons to aid you in your quest. Use them wisely, for they are powerful tools that must be wielded with care."

Dragonwülf looked down at the weapons before him and his titanium suit, marveling at their sleek design and advanced technology. He knew that with these weapons at his disposal, he would be a formidable force against anyone who sought to harm the realm.

As he prepared to leave the halls of Valhalla, Loki, the god of mischief, appeared before him, a sly smile playing on his lips. "Remember, Dragonwülf, not all threats come from without. Be wary of those who threaten from within. I would know this, because this *is my* method of operation."

Dragonwülf nodded, his jaw set in determination. "I will be vigilant, Loki. I will learn much from your example," he said tongue-in-cheek. "All the while I will always be looking over my shoulder."

Avat'or entered the chamber, asking for permission to speak.

"Oh, great Óðinn and the council of the gods, may I humbly address you?" he inquired.

"Speak, brave Avat'or, the universe owes you and the Destiny of Tyr much," said Óðinn.

"The Destiny of Tyr, a once prestigious council led by me, had made decisions that shaped the fate of entire civilizations. We were revered for our wisdom and strength, but as time passed, our influence began to fade into the annals of history. A new council is to emerge that is chosen to be the protectors of humanity and to serve until the rule of the next council."

"Great Avat'or, this is unexpected, but the council understands your wisdom," said Óðinn.

"At this time, I would choose my successor. I choose the brave Dragonwülf, a formidable warrior known for his valor in battle, as the leader," said Avat'or. "I choose his brave crew of the ship The Deepwater Watchman as the new Destiny of Tyr. I proclaim that from this day forward, they shall be known as Dragonwülf's Council of Tyr."

Dragonwülf was overcome with emotion as he spoke.

"Surely there must be another worthy to be your successor. I am not worthy."

"Indeed, you are. We have followed you all of your days, as well as all of the members of the new council. Dragonwülf the brave, you were never alone in your entire life. We were always watching and holding you up in battle. You may have felt alone, but we never left you. Your encounters with each of these heroes you are with today were appointed by The Destiny.

"I have not understood why Destiny is *called as such* until today," said an astonished Dragonwülf.

"The Destiny of the universe is now in your hands and yours alone, with the help of the new council, each chosen for their own talents and hand-picked by The Destiny. They were unable to serve in the council until all of their timelines and lives were put in order. We arranged for such a thing to happen."

Avat'or called upon each new member to stand when called.

Captain Old-Turas, a seasoned sailor with weathered skin and a troubled expression in his eyes, was chosen for his keen sense of seamanship and unwavering loyalty.

Zachariah Boyd, an everyman with a penchant for plain talk for common people, brought with him a wealth of knowledge of human nature that would prove invaluable. His skill with a sidearm will make him a valuable protector.

Jarvis Nightwish, a mysterious executioner with an acid tongue and a weapon known as the Disruptor, was known for his ability to discern truth from lies. His experience on the Saturn moon had uncovered secrets long forgotten. He was able to save his people from a vicious cult.

Viktor Vorobyev, a stoic modern paladin with a strong sense of justice, carried himself with an air of authority that demanded respect. He knows what it means to feel remorse for an evil deed and to make it right. He is being sent with what he calls a "motorcycle," which is a brave steel horse.

Sir Robert Winterfall, a noble scholar with a heart of gold and a pen that is indeed mightier than the sword, was chosen for his unwavering commitment to honor and righteousness. He will furthermore be the scribe to the Council of Tyr and the keeper of the *Obsidian Hourglass of time*. The hourglass will enable the Council to jump through the Panorama.

Luciano Cantore, a charismatic assassin with a voice of revenge, is properly placed. He brought with him tales of heroism, hope, and love. He became a figure respected not for his deadly skills but also for his sense of justice in a society absent of mercy. He received none at the hands of his brother and his La Cosa Nostra family, but he is destined to teach the world mercy.

Hansel Gru'el, known as the Harvester of Eyes, a skilled collector of eyes with a quick wit and a steady hand, was appointed for his ability to track any man and bring him to justice. He is a master of Optography, able to discern the last movements of the previous owner of a stolen eyeball.

Abraham Lincoln rounded out the new council as its most distinguished member, a humble but wise diplomat with a vision for a better world and a dream of unity among all peoples.

"All-Father Óðinn and the council of old and new gods, we present to you Dragonwülf and the Council of Tyr," announced Avat'or.

All of the gods rose to their feet out of respect for the new council.

"You will continue the work of the Destiny of Tyr, to keep peace whenever possible, to balance the fairness of warfare when war is unavoidable, and we must rid the world of the evil of war," said Avat'or.

The new members humbled and bowed before the gods as each was endowed with a small piece of the Urn of the Dead Gods that connected them with divine power from on high.

As the council gathered for its first meeting, it discussed the challenges that lay ahead. Dragonwülf pounded his fist on the table, his voice echoing through the chamber.

"We stand on the precipice of a new era, my friends," he declared. "The fate of humanity rests in our hands, and we must not falter. We are the guardians of hope, the protectors of the innocent, and the defenders of peace. Let us make a solemn vow to uphold these values with every fiber of our being."

Captain Old-Turas nodded in agreement, his weathered face creased with determination. "Aye, we shall not fail in our duty," he proclaimed. "We will weather any storm, and some bright day when the sun burns my face and bleaches my hair, I will bring the North Hundren and my crew back from the deep. I swear it."

Zachariah Boyd stroked his beard thoughtfully, "I believe we will be able to overcome the trials that await us. No one can overcome the power of good, at least not forever."

Jarvis Nightwish spoke from the shadows, his eyes glittering with mischief. "Ah, but where is the fun in that?" he quipped. "I say we keep things interesting and spice up our missions with a dash of danger and a pinch of intrigue. After all, what is life without a little excitement?"

Viktor Vorobyev crossed his arms over his chest; his expression was stern and unyielding. "Our duty has already been decided for us," he intoned. "We no longer have a choice in what we do. I promised to serve the Destiny, and *now I am* the Destiny. The road we ride is strewn with potholes and peril, but together we will finish our journey. "

Sir Robert Winterfall drew his pen from his suit jacket and, with a flourish like a sword, put it back in an imaginary scabbard. "Let us pledge ourselves to the service of humanity, and to the pursuit of knowledge," he declared. "No challenge will scare us, no enemy shall defeat us!

Hansel Gru'el cracked a smile, his eyes twinkling with mirth. "I will keep an *eye* on the horizon, scout out any trouble brewing in the wind," he offered. "You can count on me to keep us one step ahead of our enemies, to anticipate their movements."

Abraham Lincoln rose from his seat, his gaze steady and sure. "Let us remember that our strength lies not in our individual talents, but in our collective spirit," he intoned. "Together, we are invincible, united in purpose, and resolute in our resolve. Let us stand as one, against all odds, and forge a path to a brighter future for all."

Artifact Twenty-Four

Coda

Date: Future Dimension of Thor (2229 CE)

Clad in shining armor and armed with weapons of divine power, he remembered his Queen's words. He knew the weight of his sacrifice, the burden of leadership that he bore in a warrior's life.

As Dragonwülf donned the gleaming armor and wielded his newly forged weapons, he felt a surge of power, unlike anything he had ever experienced before. The gods had fashioned titanium for Morning Fire of the Sky, rendering her nearly invincible. With his heart filled with a sense of duty and purpose, Dragonwülf set out on his quest to protect the world from calamity.

Dragonwülf and Morning Fire flew out into the sky, their titanium armor gleaming in the sunlight. As they flew over the mountains and valleys, Dragonwülf felt a sense of purpose once again. With the support of Destiny and the power of his armor and weapons, he knew that he was ready to face whatever challenges lay ahead.

His first task led him to the outskirts of the forest, where he encountered a band of marauding trolls who were terrorizing the nearby villages. With a roar that shook the earth, Dragonwülf charged into battle, his titanium armor gleaming in the sunlight as he engaged the trolls in fierce combat.

"Stand back, foul creatures, for Dragonwülf has arrived to vanquish you!" he bellowed, his voice echoing through the forest.

The trolls, taken aback by the sight of the armored warrior, hesitated for a moment before launching themselves at him with wild abandon. Dragonwülf was prepared, his movements swift and precise as he dodged their attacks and struck back with deadly accuracy.

"Is that all you have?" Dragonwülf taunted, his sword flashing in the sunlight as he dispatched troll after troll with ease.

As the battle raged on, Dragonwülf's strength seemed boundless, his titanium armor deflecting the trolls' blows as if they were mere pinpricks. With a final, thunderous blow, Dragonwülf felled the last of the trolls, his breath coming in ragged gasps as he surveyed the battlefield.

The villagers who had witnessed the battle emerged from their hiding places, their faces filled with awe and gratitude. "You have saved us, Dragonwülf," they cried, kneeling before him in reverence.

Dragonwülf raised a hand to silence them, a wry smile playing on his lips. "It was my duty to protect the innocent from harm," he said solemnly, his voice filled with conviction.

Dragonwülf continued on his journey, his titanium armor gleaming in the sunlight as he set out to vanquish any foe that threatened the world he held dear. His legend grew with each passing battle, his name whispered in hushed tones by those who sought to invoke his protection.

Artifact Twenty-Five
Doomsday

Date: Future Dimension of Thor (2429 CE)
Remnants of Earth post WW4

"I am Adam."

Doomsday loomed on the horizon. Dragonwülf had warned his fellowship and those in his army in the distant past that someday all bonds of fellowship would be crushed, and humanity would cease to sing the songs of love and abandon each other. This day had come.

The world knew it was coming. It was bound to happen. The world had ended. The fellowship of man disappeared, and in its place was destruction and misery. Love of politics had taken its toll on the world. The forked-tongued, honey-dripping lies of world leaders and warring factions within the planet had come to a culmination with the war of the year 2429. The fools had left nothing in the wake of the war. The greedy and vicious animals of the world sought to kill, steal, and destroy. The rich and the politicians of the earth let them do it.

The lonely man, his footsteps echoing softly in the silent landscape, walked aimlessly through the remnants of what once was a bustling city. His eyes, empty and haunted, scanned the desolation stretching out before him. Buildings lay in ruins, cars overturned and abandoned, a ghost planet frozen in time.

Silent and mute, he was the only man left standing in a world that had crumbled around him. Not knowing how or why he had been spared while others perished, a heavy weight of guilt and confusion settled deep within his soul.

"Was I chosen to bear witness to the end?" he whispered to the wind, his voice barely more than a breath. "Why am I the only survivor?"

As he wandered, memories of the cataclysm that had befallen the world flashed before his eyes - the blinding light, the deafening roar, the overwhelming sense of helplessness as everything he knew was torn asunder.

"I wander alone," he muttered to himself, the words bitter on his tongue. "Cursed with a second life? Why me?"

The sun dipped below the horizon, casting long shadows across the wasteland. The man stood alone, a silhouette against the dying light, his heart heavy with the knowledge of his solitude.

As if driven by some unseen force, he threw back his head and let out a primal scream that tore the air in two like the ancient temple in Jerusalem. The sound echoed off the broken buildings, a cry of anguish and despair that spoke of the depths of panic and grief. "Why?" screamed the man.

In the darkness that followed, he sank to his knees, tears mingling with the dust and grime on his face. "My family ...all gone," he whispered with emotion. "There must be one who will come to save me... and to save this world."

The wind whispered through the ruins, carrying his words away into the night. As he wept, the man knew that he carried a burden heavier than any he had ever known - the burden of being the last, the only one left to bear witness to the world that had been lost. Adam trudged wearily through the desolate streets, filled with despair and uncertainty. The once bustling city now lay in ruins, covered in a thick layer of ash that obscured the remnants of civilization.

As he wandered aimlessly, his mind filled with memories of a time long gone, He spotted a church in the distance. Despite his skepticism of religion, he found himself drawn to the building, perhaps out of a sense of curiosity but more likely desperation.

The church's facade was crumbling, and the sign above the entrance was barely legible. It read,

"Trust in the Lord with all your heart and lean not on your own understanding; Proverbs 3:5-6."

Adam scoffed at the words, finding little solace in the teachings of a deity that had allowed such devastation to occur.

That is a big fat lie, is it not? I wasted my breath.

Nevertheless, he pushed open the creaking door and stepped inside, the musty scent of decay filling his nostrils. The interior was dark with faded pews lining the aisles and broken stained glass windows letting in slivers of feeble light. Still, he found some odd comfort in the surroundings.

Suddenly, a voice broke the eerie silence. "Stop! Who is there?" it called out, echoing through the empty church. Adam turned to see a young woman sitting at the altar, her frail form shrouded in shadows and her face covered in a gas mask.

"I thought I was all alone!" she said, startled, her voice filled with tears and a sense of sadness and grief. Adam approached cautiously, his heart pounding in his chest. As they drew closer, he could make out the features of the stranger beneath the mask. It was a young woman, her eyes haunted and weary, but filled with a flicker of hope.

"What is your name?" he asked, his voice softer now, filled with a mixture of relief and curiosity.

"I am Miri," the woman replied, her gaze meeting him with a mix of wariness and curiosity. What is yours?"

"I am Adam."

"Adam, what are you doing in this busted-up place?" she said with a little humor.

Adam hesitated for a moment, the memories of the destruction and loss flooding back to him. "I was in the city when the bombs fell," he finally spoke, his voice barely above a whisper. "I saw everything I loved reduced to ashes. And now, I am trying to survive as best as I can."

"How are you doing with that?" she asked.

"Not so good, I think. I have been overwhelmed by just too much…"

"Too much what?" asked Miri.

"Just too much of everything," he said, "The world has filled my eyes with too much to fear, too much mourning, too much pain, so it is hard for me to write it all down. I used to be a reporter for a news station…somewhere…I do not even remember. You know, just to keep people who survived after the War up to date on… nothing, I guess. There is no use now, I think."

Miri nodded in understanding, her own eyes reflecting the pain and loss that had shaped their existence. "We are survivors even if we don't want to be," she said softly. "I don't know if I can do this."

"I think *I* can," said Adam pensively.

The pair forged an unlikely bond amidst the ruins of the once-great city. They scavenged for food and supplies, braving the dangers that lurked in the shadows and the memories that haunted their dreams. In each other, they found solace and strength, a glimmer of hope in a world that seemed devoid of it.

They watched the sunset over the broken skyline, casting a golden glow over the shattered remnants of their past lives. Adam and Miri knew that they were not alone in their struggle.

As they sat amidst the ruins, the sun setting in a smoggy sky above them, they spoke of the world that had been lost, of the lives that had been taken in the blink of an eye. They shared stories of their past, of loved ones who were no more, finding solace in the shared experience of grief and loss.

Amidst the darkness, a glimmer of hope emerged in their conversation. Rumors had spread before the nuclear winter of a coming savior, a beacon of light in a world consumed by shadows.

"Do you believe in this savior?" Miri's voice was filled with a mix of doubt and longing. Adam hesitated, his gaze turning towards the horizon where the sun dipped below the crumbling skyline.

"You mean… like a god?"

"No, this is different, haven't you heard?" she said.

"I can't think of any other savior," he said.

"Some call it 'The great dragon from the sky," she said with a hopeful tone.

"A dragon? That is ridiculous. Who in their right mind would believe such a thing?" He stopped short when he realized she was a believer in this mysterious dragon.

"I am sorry, I do want to believe," he finally spoke, his words carrying the weight of a world that had lost all hope. "I want to believe that there is still a chance for us, for humanity, to rise from the ashes and build something new, but it seems too far-fetched."

As the night fell around them, the two sat in silence, the remnants of a broken world stretching out before them. In the darkness, they found a glimmer of hope, a shared belief in the possibility of a future yet unwritten. As they huddled together, two survivors in a world that had been torn asunder, they clung to each other and the fragile promise of a coming savior, a light in the darkness that could guide them toward a new dawn.

As the two slept intertwined, Dragonwülf and the crew of the Deepwater Watchman, many miles above the Earth, stood as sentries to this world.

The enemy of Dragonwülf, the Götterdämmerung, was still floating as a hungry wolf near a pen of sheep. The Defiler was gone, but not his spirit. The demon ship could plunder a planet to make their own, but first, they would have to plunder the Council of Tyr and Dragonwülf.

Artifact Twenty- Six

The Lost Souls of the Götterdämmerung
Dimension of Thor (Circa 2446)

"WE COME IN PEACE."

Maz'Gul rose to the top of the prison hierarchy upon the defeat of The Defiler and the death of Ogor the Impaler. He and other prisoners repaired the Götterdämmerung and flew swiftly from the galaxy without even being pursued.

"This will be our new home where we will make the rules and mete out punishment and terror at will," screamed Maz'Gul at the cowering prisoners. "From this day forward, this ship will be called The Caligulis. No longer will we be prisoners of this galaxy! Soon, the entire galaxy will be our prisoners."

The alarm blared throughout the dark, cramped corridors of the Caligulis. Chaos erupted as prisoners stormed from their quarters, their eyes filled with both fear and determination. Among them were all the former prisoners of the gulag Caligulis Q3, once a feared prison in the far reaches of the galaxy. The ship was several thousand kilometers above the Earth's atmosphere. As the ship made several orbits around the Earth, it collided with some early 21st-century space debris, causing the ship to be knocked off course.

"We are losing altitude, my lord!" said a prisoner to Maz'Gul. The prisoner was aware that any disrespect or perception of it would result in death, so he lowered his eyes and referred to Maz'Gul as 'my lord.'

"What happened?" screamed Maz'Gul to the prisoner.

"Sp- Sp- Space trash my liege, I mean Sire,"

'Go and throw yourself into the rubbish chute with the rest of the refuse at once," ordered Maz'Gul

The Caligulis plummeted through the atmosphere of Earth. The crewmembers, a ragtag group of outlaws and misfits, braced themselves as the ship rattled and groaned its hull glowing red-hot from the intense heat of re-entry.

"This is it, you maggots!" Captain Maz'Gul barked over the chaotic din. "Brace for impact! Today we die a glorious death!"

The ship shuddered violently, causing alarms to blare and sparks to fly. The prisoners shouted and screamed in terror as they felt the vessel hurtling towards the Earth's surface.

With a deafening crash, the Caligulis slammed into the ground, skidding across the rocky terrain before coming to a stop, smoke billowing from its twisted metal frame. Miraculously, the crew survived the crash landing, though the ship seemed beyond repair.

As the dust settled, the prisoners could see that they were stranded on a devastated industrial wasteland of a planet, with towering cliffs and swirling purple clouds overhead. The air was thick with an acrid scent, and strange, otherworldly creatures skittered in the shadows.

Above them, the Winterhawk circled in the sky.

"Looks like we're in for a long walk," Maz'Gul said grimly, drawing his dagger. "Stay sharp and stay together."

The crew emerged from the wreckage, blinking against the harsh sunlight, and began their journey across the landscape. They trudged through the rocky terrain of Earth, an industrial world covered in steel and steel manufacturing plants as far as the eye could see.

The crew saw an opportunity in the planet's vast resources and set out to conquer it, using their skills and ingenuity to build weapons of mass destruction that would rival even the most powerful empires in the universe. "We will be invincible!" said Maz'Gul.

"We need to find shelter and gather supplies," suggested a prisoner, scanning the horizon for any signs of life.

Suddenly, a group of creatures emerged from the shadows, their shimmering scales reflecting the strange light of the planet. Maz'Gul raised his hand, signaling the crew to hold their fire. The people known as the Q99 were refugees to Earth from their world, which was left in destruction. They had made a planetary immigration treaty with the last President of the United States of America before the country was devastated in war.

"We come in peace," Maz'Gul called out.

The creatures chirped and chattered amongst themselves before one of them stepped forward, its large eyes curious and unthreatening.

"We mean no harm. We are just stranded travelers in need of assistance," The Captain explained, with a little less sincerity in his voice.

The creatures seemed to understand, gesturing towards the horizon. The crew followed their new guides towards a hidden settlement nestled in the cliffs.

The settlement on Earth was a marvel of architecture, with crystalline structures glinting in the strange light of the planet. The crew was welcomed with curious stares and cautious smiles, their hosts offering food and shelter for the night.

The crew gathered around a crackling fire, swapping stories and sharing provisions with their alien hosts to keep them occupied. Outside Maz'Gul, a few of his trusted advisors spoke in low tones.

"We have hit the jackpot, crew, "Maz'Gul exclaimed, his voice tinged with excitement. "Let us gather all the provisions we can find and make it quick. We don't want any surprises from the locals."

The crew dispersed, their metallic boots clanking against the ground as they moved swiftly through the vibrant forests of Earth. The newer inhabitants of the planet, the Q99, a peaceful and advanced species, watched in fearful trepidation.

One of the crewmembers, a young engineer named Kael, hesitated as he saw the terror in the eyes of the inhabitants.

"Captain, isn't this going too far? These beings don't deserve this."

The Captain turned to face Kael, his expression cold and unyielding. "We take what we need and what we want, Kael. That is the law of the galaxy. If you cannot stomach what we are about to do, then perhaps you are in the wrong company of men and need to be eliminated."

Kael clenched his fists in frustration but said nothing more as he resumed his tasks, his heart heavy with guilt. The crew worked tirelessly, loading their ship with provisions stolen from the planet's inhabitants. As the last crate was sealed, Maz'Gul gave the order.

The crew carried out the Captain's orders without hesitation, their weapons firing with deadly accuracy as the peaceful beings of Q99 fell one by one. The air was filled with the sounds of rifle blasts, machine gun fire, and agonized cries, a stark contrast to the once serene atmosphere of the planet.

Once the deed was done, the crew boarded the Caligulis, their ship heavy with stolen goods and their hearts heavy with the weight of their sins.

"The caverns on the surface and our ship will be our home until we become invincible to defeat," said Maz'Gul. "We have much work to do! Work hard, and you will be rewarded. Work poorly, and I will kill you myself. We will never be anyone's prisoners again!"

Deep in the *Catacombs of Tranquility,* miles below in the underground of a Q99 settlement, a peaceful monk prayed for the deliverance of his people.

"Oh, holy one, hear my prayer. Deliver us out of the hands of these fiends and protect us so that no more death will come to my people. Surely, there will be a savior for our land. Someone must save us and deliver us from destruction. He must live. I feel it in my heart."

In another time and in another realm, that heart of steel beats as a death knell to those who would do evil. Outside of the Catacombs, the *Winterhawk* circled above in the sky.

He lives indeed.

Next in series:
Dragonwülf Book IV The Shatthererd Heavens

Acknowledgments

FRIENDS OF DRAKWNÚLFR

Kára María Fagr (Kára Marie the Fair). Karen Marie DeBella (Lady Dragonwülf)

Dragon's Den Books, Arcadia, Florida

Barnes & Noble, 71st Street, Tulsa.

Tulsa Technology Center Riverside Campus/ Kim Streater

Joe Bouchard

The music of Blue Öyster Cult

Rob Halford and the music of Judas Priest/ Invincible Shield

The music of Antti Martikainen

The Estate of JRR Tolkien

Rivendell Books in Broken Arrow, OK.

Astrid and Eric Pensa

Two Steps from Hell & the Epic Music of Thomas Bergersen

Dean and Martha Oglesby

Dr. Paul Cochran

Doug and Christie Friend

Floor Jansen and Nightwish

Dr. Paul Cochran

Doug and Christie Friend

Floor Jansen and Nightwish

And of course,

 Professor John Ronald Reuel Tolkien

Illustrations by CANVA

Salvatore DeBella is the author of the *Dragonwülf* saga, an epic fantasy series blending Norse mythology, cosmic warfare, and brutal heroism. Drawing inspiration from classic sword-and-sorcery authors such as R.A. Salvatore, DeBella creates worlds where gods bleed, dragons burn the heavens, and destiny is both a curse and a calling.

His debut novel, *Dragonwülf Book I: The Destiny of Tyr*, was published in December 2023, followed by *Dragonwülf Book II: Twilight of the Gods* and the third volume of the series in 2025, *Dragonwülf Book III: The Age of Metal*. The series has become known for its relentless action, dark mythological themes, and cinematic scope that stretches from ancient battlefields to the farthest reaches of the cosmos.

When he is not forging legends and shattering pantheons, DeBella lives in Glenpool, Oklahoma, where he continues to expand the *Dragonwülf* universe and explore new tales of fallen gods, eternal warriors, and the fragile balance of creation.

Next in the Series Book III *The Age of Metal*

Dragonwülf Book IV The Shattered Heavens

Salvatore DeBella, often known as "Sal," is an American author and public speaker specializing in epic fantasy and science fiction with a modern twist.

Literary Work:

He is best known for the Dragonwülf series, which he describes as a "cinematic fusion" of Norse mythology and futuristic elements. The trilogy includes:

(2022): His debut novel centers on an ancient civilization discovered in the 19th century and an ancient warrior named Wolfclaw.

(2024) Dragonwülf Book II: Twilight of the Gods Continues the saga of rising warriors and falling gods.

(2025)Dragonwülf Book III: The Age of Metal

To be released in 2026, Dragonwülf Book IV: The Shattered Heavens

Style and Influences

Writing Philosophy: DeBella aims for an immersive, movie-like reading experience. He often uses the term "Interdimensional Synchrony" to describe his blend of genres.

Influences: His work is heavily influenced by Edgar Allan Poe, J.R.R. Tolkien, the progressive rock band Blue Öyster Cult, and fantasy legend R.A. Salvatore.

Salvatore' DeBella

Background and Personal Life

Education and Career: Born in Pittsfield, Massachusetts, he holds a Bachelor of Arts in English Education with an emphasis in English Literature from Northeastern State University. He spent his career as a college instructor before turning to writing in 2015.

Residency: He currently lives in Glenpool, Oklahoma, with his wife, Karen.

Author Page (E-mail, etc.)

saldebella@gmail.com

Webpage
https://saldebella.wixsite.com/website

Facebook Page
https://www.facebook.com/sal.debella.7

Twitter

https://twitter.com/sal_debella